# DOG TAGS

# DOG TAGS

Dale set the letter down and sat in silence. "Have I really signed Scout up to go to war and leave me forever?" Scenes from the newsreel of a dog dodging enemy fire flashed through his mind.

Tears filled Dale's eyes, and his mother put her arms around him, whispering in his ear, "Remember, a dog like Scout saved your Dad's life." She gave him a hug. "You're doing a brave thing. Your father would be proud of you. In fact, we're all proud of you."

Book Two

# Dog Tags

## A YOUNG MUSICIAN'S SACRIFICE DURING WWII

PAUL KIMPTON

AND

ANN KACZKOWSKI KIMPTON

GIA Publications, Inc.
Chicago

**Dog Tags**

Paul Kimpton and Ann Kaczkowski Kimpton

Cover art, design, illustration, and layout by Martha Chlipala
Cover art adapted from: http://www.flickr.com/photos/medicalmuseum/302919026/flicker.
com, otisarchives1's photostream an unoffical home for public domain photographs from the
National Museum of Health & Medicine.

GIA Publications, Inc.

7404 S Mason Ave

Chicago IL 60638

www.giamusic.com

G-8093

ISBN: 978-1-57999-850-9

*For our parents who instilled in us a love*
*of music,*
*the outdoors,*
*and adventure*

*For Gregg Sewell, our wise GIA editor.*

*For the Adventures in Music Early Readers Club and*
*their suggestions.*

*This book is dedicated to all of the families that donated*
*their dogs to the Dogs for Defense Program during*
*World War II.*

# DOG TAGS

Chapter 1

# EXCITEMENT BUILDS

Dale felt the cool breeze on his face as he coasted his bike down Simpson Hill with his dog Scout galloping faithfully beside him. It had been just two weeks since the celebration in the town square honoring Dale and his friend, Charlie. Dale could still hear the call of his bugle as he rode through the streets of Libertyville, alerting the volunteer firemen of the fire at the Conn instrument factory. Neighbors and people he didn't even know continued to thank him and shake his hand for saving the factory and the nearby Air Force base.

Dale rounded the corner onto Main Street on his way to pick up Charlie at the fire station. He spied Mr. Valentine, the milkman, waving at him to stop. Mr.

Valentine delivered milk to the houses in Libertyville in a wagon that was pulled by his horse, Buddy.

"Dale, come," he said in his thick Italian accent. "How's the town's hero doing?" Mr. Valentine, a short man with black hair and thick eyebrows, pulled on Buddy's reigns and brought the wagon to a halt.

Dale enjoyed seeing Mr. Valentine and Buddy because he always got to feed the horse a treat. That morning he could see an apple in Mr. Valentine's hand as the milkman climbed down from the wagon. Dale pulled his bike up next to Buddy and patted the stocky draft horse. "Hey, Mr. Valentine. How're you doing?"

"Fine, fine. Come and take this apple for Buddy before he gets crabby." Buddy flicked his tail and perked his ears in anticipation of a treat.

"It looks like you got an early start today. I usually don't see you and Buddy at this time of day," Dale said as he held the apple up to the horse's soft muzzle.

"I heard it was going to be hot today, and thought I would get my route done before noon." Mr. Valentine took out his red handkerchief and dabbed his forehead. He bent down to scratch Scout, who had rubbed up against his knee. "Has Mr. Greenleaf delivered the new school band instruments that he promised at the ceremony?"

"Not yet, but they should be coming soon. All of the sixth graders are excited to be starting instruments."

"I'm sure they are. If I see him this morning when I deliver milk to his house, I'll ask him how much longer it'll be."

"Thanks," Dale said. "I'd better get going. I need to get to the firehouse to pick up Charlie and tie up Scout before school."

"Don't you mean P. J.?" The milkman laughed and climbed back into the wagon.

Dale smiled and waved goodbye. He remembered how Charlie had ridden through the streets in his pajamas as Dale played the Fire Call on his bugle. He could still hear the crowd at the ceremony chanting, "P. J., P. J." as he pulled up to the firehouse. Scout ran up to Smokey, the firehouse dog, and sniffed to greet him as Charlie bounded out the door.

"What took you so long? I was afraid we were going to be late."

"I'm sorry, but I stopped to talk to Mr. Valentine and feed Buddy an apple. Do you believe he remembered your nickname—P. J.—from the ceremony?"

"Who doesn't remember it?" Charlie said, turning red and speaking louder. "That's all anyone calls me."

"Come on, Charlie. It's a great nickname, and one you'll have forever." Dale gently punched his friend on the shoulder.

"Lucky me! Let's tie up these dogs and get to school."

On the way, Dale and Charlie tried to see who could ride the farthest without using their hands. They both had ridden four blocks, and as they rounded the last corner, the boys spotted their friends waiting for them at the bike rack next to the playground.

Victor chanted, "P. J., P. J." Then Tommy, Dave, Bobby, and Karl joined in. "P. J., P. J."

Charlie was in the lead when he heard the chant. He jerked his head, and the bike began to swerve. He desperately tried to keep his balance, but the bike veered into the curb, tossing him onto the grass. He looked up as Dale coasted up to the bike rack, his hands still in the air.

"That's not fair," Charlie shouted as he brushed grass and dirt from his pants. "Do you know how mad my mom would've been if I'd torn my new pants?"

Tommy said, "Do you really want to tell your mom you were riding without your hands?" Everyone laughed as Dale and Charlie put the bikes in the rack for the day.

Dale turned. "I thought you had me for a minute back there."

"I would have if Victor hadn't distracted me by chanting my new nickname."

"I like P.J. I don't think you understand how cool it is. Kind of like Babe Ruth is the Great Bambino. Think of other famous people who have nicknames. The greatest football player ever, Harold "Red" Grange, is the Galloping Ghost. My hero, Louis Armstrong, is known everywhere as Satchmo. Of course, we all know Slim down at the fire station. You should be proud to have a name people will remember."

Charlie wiped the sweat from his forehead. "Wow, I guess I never thought of it that way. OK, from now on, you can call me P. J."

As the boys walked up to the doors of Emerson School, Chrissy and Bridget caught up to them. "Are you all right, Charlie?" Bridget said as she plucked a piece of grass from Charlie's shoulder. Chrissy chimed in. "We saw you crash your bike into the curb." She put her arms around him and gave him a hug. Charlie turned bright red, and everyone laughed. "It's nothing," he said, standing up tall. Then he looked Chrissy in the eye and said, "You can call me P. J."

Dale opened the door for the girls. "Ladies first."

"You're such a gentleman," Bridget said as she lightly touched his hand.

Bobby slid in behind the girls and in a high-pitched voice added, "Oh, Dale, you're such a gentleman." The other boys shoved through the door after Bobby, laughing as Dale stood holding the door.

Mrs. Cooper, who had been watching, came to the rescue. "That was very nice of you, Dale. Now come along and get to class."

It was Friday, and all of the students were excited about the upcoming weekend. Mrs. Cooper had to use her loud voice to get her everyone's attention. She pointed to the math assignment on the board and asked the class to get out their books and paper. As they began working on the problems, Dale felt Chrissy poke him in the back with her pencil. Not wanting to get in trouble, he ignored the jabs. Then she poked him even harder. Dale whipped around to say something, only to see her pointing out the window at a large truck pulling up into the alley by the auditorium. On the side of the truck was painted Conn Instruments in bright red letters.

Without hesitation Dale said, "The new instruments are here," and he bolted to the window. All of the students followed, even Mrs. Cooper.

The teacher, having realized what she had done, said, "Well, I guess we're all as excited as Dale. Let's move back to our seats and continue the lesson."

The minutes dragged on. Dale had a hard time focusing on his math assignment. "Could this be the truck with the new instruments?" he thought.

The classroom door squeaked. Dale looked up to see Mr. Prenty, the principal, enter the room and whisper something in Mrs. Cooper's ear. The student's eyes were locked on the two adults, hoping to hear what they were discussing. Finally, Dale heard the teacher say, "Well, if you think this is more important than math, you may take them with you."

Mr. Prenty cleared his throat. "The new band instruments have just arrived. After talking to Mrs. Cooper and assuring her that all of you understand the importance of your math assignment, I'd like to have the following students come with me to the auditorium. Mr. Jeffrey is waiting for you to help him unload the truck and take inventory of the new instruments." A murmur of excitement rose. "Dale, since you and your friend Charlie, or should I say P. J., are responsible for this donation, I'd like you and seven others to come with me."

Dale felt another jab from behind. He turned and Chrissy motioned for her and Bridget to be included.

Mr. Prenty said, "I've asked Mrs. Cooper to bring the rest of the class down later to see the instruments and hear about the new band program. This is a great day for Emerson School."

The whole class began clapping as Dale and P. J. stood up to select the ones to help. "I'd like Victor and Bobby," Dale said. The two boys ran to join him and P. J. at the front of the room. P. J. said, "I want Karl and Dave." Chrissy looked like she was about ready to cry when Dale said, "And Bridget." His eyes scanned the eager class for one more person to help. "And how about Chrissy?" Chrissy jumped up and joined the other students at the front of the room.

They followed Mr. Prenty to the auditorium where Mr. Jeffrey was waiting. "We'll need to unload each instrument carefully and write down the serial numbers." Mr. Jeffrey led them to the backstage door where the truck had pulled up to the loading dock.

"What's a serial number?" Dave said.

"Well, each instrument has its own number stamped on it. That number is never duplicated. The serial number is used to keep track of the instruments. The numbers tell the year and month and how many instruments were made. Since instruments may look the same, we can also figure out who the instrument belongs to if we know the serial number."

The rest of the day was spent unloading flutes, clarinets, oboes, bassoons, saxophones, trumpets, French horns, trombones, tubas, and percussion instruments. Once Mr. Jeffrey showed them where the serial numbers were stamped and how to handle each instrument, the process went quickly. The boys unloaded the instrument cases, and the girls opened the cases and read the serial numbers to Mr. Jeffrey. After a couple of hours of work, the students sat down on the stage and admired the brand new, shiny instruments. Mr. Jeffrey said, "Dale, why don't you ask Mrs. Cooper to bring the rest of the students to the auditorium?" Dale dashed back to the classroom.

He soon returned, and the class sat in the front rows. The band teacher smiled at the eager faces. "The sixth grade band program will start next week. Over the weekend, I'd like you to think about what instrument you would like to play. I understand that your music teacher, Mrs. Vincent, has taught you the names of the instruments and what they sound like. After you tell me what you'd like to play, I'll look at your hands, fingers, teeth, and lips to see if that's the best instrument for you. I want you to play something that matches your strengths." Everyone began whispering and pointing at the instruments on the tables lining the stage.

"Please take one of these sheets and mark the three instruments you want to play. Return it to me on Monday. Now I'll have the first row come up on stage. You can look, but don't touch; you'll get to do that next week."

The students walked around the tables discussing what instruments they wanted to play while Dale and the gang stood to the side. Dale turned to the girls. "I know it's Friday, and we always race after school, but can we skip it this week? I want to go home right away."

Chrissy winked at Bridget. "OK, but next Friday the race is back on." Her ponytail flipped as she turned to look at the instruments again.

After the students had circled the tables several times, Mrs. Cooper hustled them back to the classroom. As the bell rang, the sixth graders bounded out the door of the school. Dale and P. J. made their way through the crowd to the bike rack where the gang was waiting.

"Let's not go to the Jungle today," Bobby said, referring to the empty lot that served as the boys' play area. "I want to talk to my parents about the instrument

I'm going to play."

Victor agreed. "Let's meet at the movies tomorrow." The boys got on their bikes and pedaled away in different directions.

Dale and P. J. rode to the firehouse, discussing the new instruments and what everyone was going to play. Scout and Smokey barked in greeting as the boys skidded to a stop. Dale untied Scout, who jumped up to lick his face.

"See you tomorrow at the movies—eleven o'clock sharp," P. J. said.

Dale peeled out with Scout in pursuit. He pedaled up Simpson Hill and thought about the stories he would share at the dinner table. It was Friday, and Grandma would serve her thick-battered fried chicken with homemade noodles. "Let's hurry, Scout. I'm hungry."

Chapter 2

# TOUGH CHOICE

The next morning Dale rolled over in bed and rubbed his eyes. He had been dreaming about flying, and the sound of roaring engines seemed so real. His eyes blinked and the low growl of the engines continued. Then Dale realized the sound wasn't coming from his dream, but from outside his window. He jumped up, ran down the stairs and onto the front porch. Craning his neck and shielding his eyes, Dale searched the sky for planes. Scout, who had been sleeping under the porch, ran up and rubbed against his leg.

Dale spotted several black specks on the horizon of a cloudless blue sky. Scout began barking as the specks grew larger, and the ground began to shake from the vibration of the engines. A formation of six B-25 Mitchell bombers came into focus. They banked and headed straight for Dale's house. As they approached, Dale jumped up and down, waving his hands in the air. The planes roared over the house at treetop level and waggled their wings in greeting, zooming past Dale.

As the sound faded, Dale remembered that at dinner the night before his mother said she was flying with a group of bombers to Dayton, Ohio, where they would be sent to the Pacific. The United States was at war with both Germany and Japan, and shipped bombers to both fronts. Mother explained that the plane she was flying was the same type of bomber used in the film *Thirty Seconds over Tokyo* that Dale and his friends were going to see. The movie was about the true story of Lieutenant Colonel James "Jimmy" Doolittle's raid on Japan in 1941, just four months after the Japanese had attacked Pearl Harbor. She said the story was written by Captain Ted W. Lawson, one of seventeen pilots who participated in the raid and had lived to tell the story. Dale remembered every detail of her story and could not wait to tell the gang when he got to the movie.

He ran up the steps, flung open the screen door and raced into the kitchen. Grandpa Rodine was reading the paper and drinking a cup of steaming black coffee.

Dale inhaled the smell of the coffee. "Can I have my usual Saturday cup of coffee?"

Grandma wiped her hands on her apron. "Don't you mean, '*May* I have my usual Saturday cup of coffee?'"

"May I, please?" Dale said as he sat down. Grandma poured, mixed in some frothy cream, and placed the cup in front of Dale. He breathed in the pungent smell.

"Your mom must have waked you and all of Libertyville this morning."

"That was swell. And to think the bombers are the same as the ones in the movie I'm seeing today."

Grandpa sipped his coffee. "I remember hearing about Jimmy Doolittle and his dangerous mission on the radio. Because of men like him, the war may be over soon."

Dale swirled his spoon in his coffee. "If the war does end, then Dad can come home for good." He stared into his cup. "I miss him a lot."

"We all do," Grandma said sitting next to Dale. "But enough war talk. Why don't you tell your Grandpa about the new instruments that arrived at school yesterday?" Grandpa had missed the usual family dinner because he had to run a freight train to Chicago.

"You wouldn't believe how excited everyone is." And for the next half hour, Dale and Grandpa discussed yesterday's excitement.

Grandpa scratched his chin. "So, are you going to play the gold-plated cornet that Mr. Greenleaf gave to you for saving the Conn factory?"

"Absolutely. I'm taking it to school on Monday."

"Well, once your teacher gives you the OK, it'll be fun for us to learn the cornet together, just like we learned the bugle."

Dale finished his breakfast and brought his dishes to the sink. "I'd better get dressed. I have to meet the gang at eleven o'clock sharp."

"Run along," Grandma said. "I'll have lunch waiting for you after the movie."

Five minutes later Dale was dressed and dashing out the front door with Scout in pursuit. On the porch, Dale bent down and patted his dog. "Sorry, Scout. Today, you have to stay here until after the movie." Scout's ears fell and he stopped wagging his tail. He twisted his head and looked at his master.

"Come on, Scout. I won't be gone too long. After the movie, I'll take you to the Jungle, and you can play Army with us." Scout's ears and tail perked up at the word *Jungle,* and he watched patiently as Dale pedaled away.

As he turned the corner to ride down Simpson Hill, Dale spied Chrissy and Bridget walking ahead. Dale leaned forward on his bike and raced up behind the two girls. He slammed on his brakes at the last minute. Both girls screamed and jumped onto the grass at the skidding sound.

"Gotcha!" Dale teased as the girls turned to face him.

Once they realized it was Dale, they laughed. "You scared us half to death sneaking up on us like that," Chrissy said.

"That'll teach you not to pay attention when you're walking next time. Are you two going to the movie this morning?"

"No, we're going to Swan's Records to get the new Andrews Sisters song, 'Boogie Woogie Bugle Boy,'" Bridget said. "My dad heard they're going to do a USO show at the Air Force base next month with the Tommy Dorsey Jazz Orchestra."

Dale nodded. "I know that song. It starts with a bugle call. I've heard it on the radio. My mom calls it 'jump blues' or music you can dance to." Dale snapped his fingers as he hummed the opening bugle call.

Then his eyes widened, "Since my mom works at the base, maybe I can talk her into getting us tickets."

Chrissy grabbed Bridget's hands and they both jumped up and down. "You mean you can get us tickets, for real?"

"I think so. I'll ask my mom at dinner tonight," he said as he pushed off on his bike.

As Dale pulled up to the bike rack next to the theatre, the gang was already in line. Victor was running up and down with his arms out, buzzing his lips and pretending to shoot down enemy aircraft. When Victor saw Dale, he turned and ran straight at him, making the sound of machine guns firing. Dale raised his arms and began shooting back at Victor before crashing to the ground. Victor flew past to his place in line, shouting, "Take that, Red Barron."

Dale got up, dusted off his jeans and cut in line next to P. J. "Victor sure can make a great machine gun sound."

Dave sighed and rolled his eyes. "He's been doing that for the last ten minutes." The line began to inch forward.

P. J. said, "Was that your mom in one of the bombers this morning?" Dale nodded as the boys placed their money on the ticket counter and entered the theater.

They found an empty row and settled into worn velvet seats. The lights of the chandelier dimmed, sending a wave of excitement through the crowd that slowly stopped bobbing up and down. A kernel of popcorn arched over the aisles and landed on the wooden stage, bringing a loud laugh from the audience. As the heavy red curtains parted, ripples of velvet flowed across the stage until the folds framed an enormous ivory screen. A rectangle of light appeared, projecting a magnified strand of hair and dust on the screen. Gradually a picture of a spinning globe came into focus. The Saturday matinee had finally begun.

Dale curled his knees under him and leaned forward so he could see around the fuzzy-haired girl in front of him. He was anxious to see the movie.

The girl in front of Dale shifted to the right. Dale leaned to the left so he could see around her. Usually the opening newsreel focused on stories of World War II. Since 1941, America had been preoccupied with fighting two wars, one in the Pacific where Dale's father was stationed and the other in Europe.

Before the bombing of Pearl Harbor in Hawaii, Americans had felt safe from direct enemy attack. Pearl Harbor had changed all that. Dale watched wide-eyed as the announcer's voice boomed over the picture of a foggy, deserted beach. "On June 13, 1942, eight German spies slipped into the United States from a submarine off the Atlantic coast. The spies have since been rounded up, but the point remains that patrolling our coast with men alone is an impossible job. To keep America safe, we need the help of our canine companions."

A snarling Doberman Pinscher strained at his leash and growled at the audience as his military handler demonstrated how dogs were being trained to sniff out enemy spies, guard munitions factories, and help our troops in battle.

"Dogs are vital in combat. As you can see, this brave dog is carrying important military messages from a unit that is without radio contact and is surrounded."

The audience cheered as the dog dodged shellfire and zigzagged his way from the stranded army unit hiding in thick jungle vegetation. The dog's message, hidden in his special leather collar, alerted the other troops to the desperate situation of the surrounded soldiers. Reinforcements were sent immediately and, thanks to the dog's heroic effort, not a single American life was lost. The scene then shifted to Washington D.C., where President Roosevelt shook the dog's paw and presented him with a set of official Army dog tags.

"Dogs are desperately needed for the war effort. Ordinary citizens can support Uncle Sam by enlisting their pets in the Dogs for Defense program. The military needs 125,000 dogs, which won't be possible without your help."

Dale's thoughts flew to Scout. He remembered his father telling about the Army dog that had saved his life. Dale could still hear his dad saying, "The military needs good dogs. Perhaps Scout could save another father's life." The words were still on Dale's mind when *Thirty Seconds over Tokyo* began. He watched the screen, but he was really thinking about Dogs for Defense, Scout, and his dad fighting somewhere in the Pacific.

When the movie ended and the lights came on, the boys lingered in their seats, talking about the movie. Finally, Tommy said, "I'm starving. Let's go to P. J.'s for some sandwiches." They jumped up and hurried outside into bright sunlight. As the boys got on their bikes, Dale said, "I'm going home to get Scout. I'll meet you at the Jungle."

Dale could hear Victor and the gang making machine gun sounds as he rode back up Simpson Hill, quietly wondering about volunteering Scout for the military.

When he got to the top of the hill, he could see Scout on the porch, his ears alert. Scout dashed to Dale as he pulled up on his bike. He jumped up on his master and licked his face. Dale took a deep breath and buried his face in Scout's black-and-white fur.

Grandmother had his peanut butter sandwich waiting for him as he entered the kitchen. During the quick lunch, Dale talked nonstop about the movie and the newsreel. When he finished his third sandwich, he patted his stomach and said, "Wow, I guess three sandwiches is my limit."

"Well, I hope so. Now off you go, and don't be late for dinner."

When Dale and Scout got to the fort, his friends were busy collecting dirt clods for grenades, sweeping and raising the flag on the pole out front.

Dale slid to a stop and admired the boys' work. "Sorry I'm late. I ate and talked too much at lunch. The place looks great."

Victor lugged a bag full of dirt grenades into the fort. "We decided that we're going to pretend we're part of Doolittle's crew. We've crash-landed in China, and now we have to escape the enemy. What do you think?"

"Great idea! Let's pretend the fort is the safe house, just like in the movie," Dale said.

The boys gathered around and P. J. said, "Dale, you can be Doolittle, and Victor can be Lawson. Bobby, Dave, and Scout can be your crew. Tommy, Smokey, and I will be the enemy. We'll try to capture you before you can get to the safe house."

"All right. Give us five minutes to hide." Dale and his team ran into the woods.

After walking a few hundred feet, Dale motioned for them to halt. "Why don't we split up into two groups and use Scout to send messages back and forth?"

Victor took out a piece of paper and some pencils. "I had these in my pocket from doing collections on my paper route."

"Swell!" Dale said. "Make sure you tuck the messages into Scout's collar like this so they don't fall out." He lifted Scout's jaw and looked him in the eye. "Can you deliver these messages safely?" Scout barked twice in response.

"Shhh. You're going to give our position away," Victor said. They heard Tommy whistle, indicating the game had begun.

"Let's split up," Dale said. "Scout, you go with Victor and Dave." Victor grabbed Scout's collar and led him to the edge of the clearing before plunging into the brush.

Bobby and Dale took off down the path in the opposite direction.

Once Victor and Dave were deep in the woods, they found a place to hide under a large pine tree. Lifting up a branch, they crawled underneath and huddled near the trunk. Victor took out the paper and pencil and wrote a message. "Going up the dry creek bed north of the fort." He rolled up the message and tucked it into Scout's collar while he whispered in the dog's ear, "Go get Dale." Scout turned his head and looked quizzically at Victor. "Go get Dale," Victor repeated. As if he understood, Scout crawled out from under the branches and took off at a dead run.

In the meantime, Dale climbed a tree to survey the area. He could see P. J. and Tommy working their way through the weeds while Smokey was happily digging a hole back at the fort. A glimpse of fur moving quickly caught Dale's eye, and he watched as Scout, who had been heading straight for the weeds where P. J. and Tommy were, suddenly stopped running and began crawling on all fours. Once Scout crawled safely past the boys, he began running with his nose to the ground. Within minutes, he was sitting at the bottom of the tree with Bobby looking up at his master. Dale smiled, climbed down and plucked the note from the dog's collar. The boys read the note.

Bobby shook his head. "They can't go to the creek.

That's where P. J. is headed. We've got to stop them."

Dale wrote another message and tucked it into Scout's collar. "Go get Victor." Once again, Scout took off into the woods.

Victor heard something approaching as he and Dave continued down the path. He held up his hand to signal Dave to stop. Slowly Scout crawled out of an opening in the weeds, wagging his tail. Dave edged over as Victor took the note from the collar and opened it. "Stop!!! Do not go to the creek! P. J. is headed that way. Meet at the bridge south of the fort!"

"Wow that was close!" Victor said as he wrote his response. After slipping the note into Scout's collar, he said, "Go get Dale," then gave the dog a pat before he took off. The two boys turned to make their way through the brush to the old stone bridge.

At first, Scout lost Dale's scent. He turned in circles and sniffed the air. Then he took off running toward a hollow tree a few hundred feet from the bridge. The dog stopped at the base of the tree and poked his head into a large knothole.

"Scout, you nearly scared me to death!" Bobby said, crawling out. Dale grabbed the note and read, "Will approach from the south—when you hear three crow calls, throw the dirt grenades. We'll rush the fort."

The minutes ticked by. In the distance, they heard, "Caw, caw, caw." Dale and Bobby readied their grenades. Bobby put his hand to his mouth and answered, "CAW, CAW!" The boys launched the grenades, which landed in the weeds directly to the right of P. J. and Tommy.

P. J. called to Tommy and Smokey. "I hear them." He ran into the weeds, pretending to shoot a machine gun. As P. J. ran, Dale, Bobby, Victor, and Dave jumped up from their hiding places and ran inside the fort, passing Smokey, who was still happily digging in the dirt.

Dale climbed onto the roof through the trap door and lowered the flag, signaling they had won. Scout barked wildly as the boys yelled, "We made it, we made it!" Hearing the celebration, P. J. and Tommy sheepishly headed back, knowing they had been tricked.

The five o'clock factory whistle blew. "All these war games make me hungry," Dale said as the boys folded the flag.

"What *doesn't* make you hungry?" Bobby said as they got on their bikes. They agreed to meet at the school bike rack Monday morning.

"Don't forget to bring your instrument selection sheet," P.J. said.

Dale thought that there was no way he would forget to bring the sheet to school. At the fire station the boys parted ways. Dale rode up the hill with Scout galloping beside him as the sky darkened. He leaned down and said. "You made me proud today. You would've made Dad proud, too." Scout barked in response. Dale took a deep breath, "I think we need to ask Mom about signing you up for Dogs for Defense."

Chapter 3

# THE MAKEOVER

Dale liked Sunday morning, which always started with a big breakfast before church. As he came downstairs, he could smell eggs, corned beef hash, and coffee. His stomach growled with hunger.

"Morning." Dale slid next to his mother, who was sitting at the table with Grandma and Grandpa.

"Well, good morning to you! You sure slept late." Grandfather swigged his coffee.

"I had a hard time going to sleep after all the talk last night about signing Scout up for Dogs for Defense."

"Are you sure you want me to make the call?" Mother said as she stood up to get Dale some eggs.

"That's why it took me so long to go to sleep. If we want this war to end, and for Dad to come home, then

Scout and I need to do our part." Mother set a plate of steaming eggs and hash in front of Dale. "Mom, can you make the call today?"

"No, it's Sunday. I'll call first thing Monday. I've met the man in charge, Captain Stonemiller. He's very nice, and I'm sure he'll find Scout a great recruit." Grandpa nodded in approval.

Dale dug his fork into the hash and gobbled his breakfast.

After breakfast and a quick change of clothes, Grandpa, Grandma, Dale, and his mother left for the short walk to church. Dale was proud because he was wearing a pair of new pants that fit him, so his friends wouldn't be able to tease him about outgrowing his pants. The family crossed the street just as Chrissy's family exited their house and joined them. Dale and Chrissy walked behind their parents so they could talk without interruption.

After a block, Dale's mom turned and said, "Why don't you tell Chrissy the news?"

"I forgot to tell you that I'm enlisting Scout in Dogs for Defense."

Mother shook her head. "No, I meant the news about the tickets."

Chrissy stopped and put her hands on her face.

"Did you get tickets to the Andrews Sisters and Tommy Dorsey concert?"

"Mom called General Packston and told him we're big fans. He told her it was the least he could do for someone who saved the Air Force base. He gave us nine tickets." Dale shyly kicked a stone on the sidewalk.

Chrissy jumped up and down and then hugged Dale, who blushed. The parents laughed as Chrissy pulled back and said, "Thanks, Mrs. Kingston! Did Dale tell you I bought a recording of 'Boogie Woogie Bugle Boy' yesterday?"

"No, but I'd love to have you bring it over before the concert. That's the song with the bugle call at the beginning, isn't it?"

"Before Chrissy could answer, Dale raised his arms like he was playing the bugle and sang out.

"I guess I was right, Dale. You'll have to play that for me," Chrissy said, and jabbed him in the shoulder.

"It won't take me long, since we're starting band on Monday."

As the walk to church continued, the conversation between Chrissy and Dale ranged from the concert to Scout, and finally to what instruments everyone was going to play.

"I can't decide between flute, French horn, and tuba."

Mr. Rule, Chrissy's dad, spun around. "*Tuba?* Where'd that idea come from?"

"Yesterday at the record store I heard some Dixieland jazz, and a tuba was playing the bass line." Chrissy looked her dad in the eye. "I loved it, so I thought it would be a fun instrument to play."

"Maybe fun, but kind of big to carry home."

"No, Mr. Jeffery told us that if we play the tuba, we get to play one at school and keep one at home. All I'd have to carry is the mouthpiece and the book."

Mr. Rule laughed. "That sounds like an option. It'll be fun to hear what Mr. Jeffrey thinks of your choices."

The families arrived at the church to the strains of organ music wafting from open windows. They scurried up the steps, opened the wooden doors, and found seats just as the service started. The pastor's sermon seemed to go on forever, but in a little over an hour the family was back at home. Grandma hustled into the kitchen to ready a roast beef. Dale's mom had to check on some planes at the Air Force base, while Grandpa lazily stretched out on the sofa for an afternoon nap.

Dale decided that if Scout was going to enlist in the Army, he first needed a bath. The silver washtub bounced and sparked as Dale dragged it along the driveway to the outside faucet in the backyard. Dale uncoiled the garden hose, put the nozzle in the tub, and turned the faucet to full blast. The nozzle banged the sides of the tub furiously like a wiggling snake trying to escape. He laughed as he tried to catch the hose, finally grabbing the end just before it flew out of the tub. One time when Dale was giving Scout a bath, the hose did the same thing but ended up smacking Scout on the snout. Scout howled and took off running down the street in pain. It took Dale and the gang over three hours to find Scout and drag him back to the house. Scout never trusted the hose or liked baths after that incident, and Dale knew he would have his hands full today trying to get Scout in the tub.

Once the tub was filled about a third of the way to the top, Dale had to find Scout and cajole him into taking a bath. Scout was usually under the porch sleeping when he was not playing with Dale. Today, however, Scout must have figured out he was getting a bath and was nowhere to be found. Dale made sure the soap and towels were ready—now all he needed was Scout. "Where could that dog have gone?" Dale searched the yard and all the usual hiding places.

Dale knew Scout rarely went in the house. He entered through the back door and peered into the living room. Sure enough, there was Scout lying on his side in the sun by the big picture window while Grandpa snored on the sofa. Dale noticed Scout's paws were making running motions as he slept. He tiptoed to Scout and stood over him. The dog lifted his head and eyed him cautiously, knowing something was up.

"Come on, Scout, we've got to get you ready for the Army," and he grabbed Scout's collar. The dog wormed his head out of the collar and was able to escape his master's grip. He leaped past Dale's snoozing Grandpa and headed for the dining room. Dale chased him twice in a circle through the house, finally cutting Scout off in the kitchen. Luckily Grandma was in the basement getting some canned jars of vegetables for dinner, so Dale escaped a reprimand. With a firm grip he dragged the dog out the back door and down the steps.

They had crossed the yard when Scout spied the dreaded tub. The dog immediately dropped his hindquarters on the ground and dug his claws into the dirt.

"Scout, you have to take a bath so you'll look nice. And besides, you stink like a dog."

The dog gingerly put one front paw in the cool water as if he were testing the temperature. Looking up at Dale through his mass of shaggy fur, he seemed to be asking if this bath were really necessary.

Seeing no means of escape, Scout climbed into the tub and sat patiently, shivering. Dale picked up a bowl, scooped up some water and poured it down the dog's back. He then took the bar of soap and rubbed it up and down Scout's straggly fur. In a matter of minutes the shaggy dog was transformed from a healthy-looking mass of fur to a skinny, soapy creature.

When Dale was satisfied that Scout would pass muster, he hosed down the beast, whose teeth were now chattering, making sure the hose did not come near Scout. He really didn't feel like chasing him again. In being careful, however, Dale lost control of the hose, and it whipped Scout on the rear end this time, causing the dog to utter a loud yelp. Before he could escape, Dale grabbed the dog. "I'm sorry, Scout... it was an accident."

Dale draped a towel over the dog. Scout helped by shaking the rest of the water from his fur right into Dale's face, and then turned to look at his master as if saying, "How does *that* feel?"

The boy laughed, picked up a brush and groomed Scout's fur until the black-and-white coat was as soft as goose down.

Dale cocked his head to one side, appraising the future recruit. Something was missing. "Ahh." He realized what Scout needed most of all—a haircut. Crew cuts were a military requirement, so why not make Scout look ready for duty?

"Sit, Scout," Dale said, then ran to get the scissors. Grandma was busy in the kitchen and did not hear him sneak into her sewing cabinet and take the scissors.

Scout watched his master cross the yard with the shiny object in his hand. Dale knew exactly what to do. He had watched Mr. Bailey cut hair when he went to his barbershop with his grandfather. Lifting up Scout's fur with two fingers, Dale cut off lock after lock. About halfway through, Dale's arms began to tire, and Scout started to whimper, "Come on, boy. Just a few more snips."

Dale tried to make the fur as even as possible, but the more he cut, the shorter it became, until it stood out all over the dog in uneven tufts about an inch long.

Grandma opened the back door. As she stepped onto the porch, she noticed little fluffs of hair rolling across the grass like tumbleweeds. She looked across the yard to see Dale rubbing a strange-looking dog with some kind of cream.

"Dale, whose dog is that? Why, what happened to Scout?"

"I hope Grandpa doesn't mind that I borrowed his Brylcreem hairdressing. That's what Mr. Bailey puts on all the men after their haircuts."

Grandma picked up the scissors and clipped a few strands to even out Scout's ragged coat. Scout stood up and shook himself, sending wisps of fur everywhere.

"Well, Dale. It looks like Scout is really ready for the Army, but I'm not sure the Army is ready for Scout's new haircut. Hopefully his fur will grow out before they come and test him. Go on, get a rake and get all that fur cleaned up before your mom gets home and dinner is ready. I think she'll be very surprised."

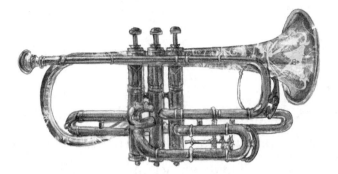

Chapter 4

# INSTRUMENT SELECTION

At breakfast the next morning, Dale was surprised to see Scout in the kitchen.

"Morning," Dale said as he reached down to pat Scout. "How come Scout is inside this morning?"

"Well, after seeing how you cut Scout's hair last night, I wanted to see if I could trim up his fur. I did the best I could." Mom tilted her head and surveyed her work.

"Sorry I cut so much off. I guess I got carried away."

"Don't worry. I'm sure Captain Stonemiller will see that Scout is an excellent candidate. I'll set up the appointment when I get to the base."

"Thanks," Dale said, and dug into his oatmeal.

"Is your cornet packed for your meeting with Mr. Jeffrey?"

"Yes, and I even shined it. I sure hope I can play cornet."

"I'm sure Mr. Jeffrey will let you. Now finish your breakfast." Grandma entered the kitchen. She looked at Dale and put her hands on her hips. "Two hands on the handlebars, young man. I don't want to hear about you riding without your hands like last Friday, do you hear me?"

"How did you know?"

Grandma winked at mother. "Dale, it's a small town, and everyone knows everything."

"Now get going. I'll be sure to call Captain Stonemiller," said his mother.

Dale headed out the door, "Come on, Scout. We don't want to be late." Scout trotted down the steps of the porch as Dale slung his knapsack with the cornet inside over his shoulders. As he rode toward the Rule house, Chrissy came out. "See you at school." Then she did a double take. "Where'd you get that dog? Where's Scout?"

"This *is* Scout. Can't you tell?"

Chrissy knelt down beside the dog. "What happened to your fur?" She looked up at Dale, "Is he sick or something?"

"He's not sick. I got a bit carried away with the scissors when I gave him a haircut."

"A little bit carried away?" Chrissy stood up and laughed. "I'll never let you cut my hair!"

Dale was anxious to change the subject.

"Did you remember your instrument selection sheet?"

Chrissy patted her purse. "Do you have yours?"

"Got it right here in my cornet case," Dale said as he took off down Simpson Hill.

He rode faster than usual, thinking, "After all the waiting I finally get to start band!"

Dale saw P. J. and Smokey waiting outside the firehouse. Scout ran ahead to meet them, but as he got closer, Smokey started growling and barking wildly. P. J. grabbed Smokey's leash to hold him back.

"Where'd you get that mangy-looking dog?"

Dale jumped off his bike and grabbed Scout, who was also growling and barking. "Smokey, it's OK, it's just Scout. Calm down!"

P. J. looked at his friend in disbelief.

"I just cut his fur a little too much is all."

The two dogs warily circled each other. When they finally had a chance to sniff one another, Smokey realized this strange-looking dog was Scout.

"That was close," P. J. said as he wiped his brow. "I thought we were going to have a dog fight on our hands."

"I guess he doesn't like strange dogs, or dogs with short hair. Let's tie them up and get going. Do you have your instrument selection sheet?"

"Sure do," P. J. said, pulling out a wrinkled form from his pocket.

He jumped on his bike and took off for school with Dale giving chase. P.J. pulled up first to the bike rack where the other boys were waiting.

"Wow, P. J., You're sweating like a pig!" Victor said, "Look at your shirt."

P. J. looked down at his wet shirt. "I hope I didn't ruin my instrument signup sheet." He reached into his pocket and took out a crumpled and soggy piece of paper.

Dale rolled up and put his bike in the rack. "What got into you, P. J.? You were riding like a madman back there."

"I don't know. I guess I'm just excited about picking an instrument. See? My sheet's not ruined." And as he held it up with two fingers, the wet sheet tore down the center. The boys laughed and headed for the school.

Tommy noticed Dale's knapsack. "What's in there?"

"That's the cornet I got from Mr. Greenleaf."

"Can we see it?" Dave said.

"No, I just shined it and don't want your fingerprints all over it."

Dave started to run. "Let's see when we get to meet with Mr. Jeffrey."

The boys pushed through the doors of Emerson School, scurried down the highly polished hallway and took their seats in Mrs. Cooper's room just as the bell rang.

The teacher entered the room and could not believe her eyes when she saw her students were in their seats. "I wish I had a camera. I don't think you've ever been to class this early and this quiet."

Dale raised his hand. "We just wanted to get here early to find out how instrument selection works."

Mrs. Cooper smiled. "Let's get started by looking at the board. You'll see that Mr. Jeffrey has written your name and the time you will report to him in the auditorium. Each appointment will take about fifteen minutes, and he'll test your musical ability. He'll ask you to match pitch, clap and repeat rhythms, buzz your lips, and sing. He'll also check your physical characteristics to see if they match your instrument choices. The last step will be to have you try the instrument before he sends you back to class."

All eyes were on Mrs. Cooper as she scanned the room. "In order to keep our minds on our schoolwork, when you return, please write next to your name what instrument you were assigned. This way we won't have everyone asking each other. Does anyone have any questions before I send the first student down?"

Everyone stared at the board, checking out what time they would meet with Mr. Jeffrey.

Chrissy poked Dale in the back. "Can you believe I'm first?"

Dale turned his head sideways. "Can you believe I'm the last one at two o'clock?"

Mrs. Cooper tapped her pencil on her book. "Chrissy, when you and Dale are done whispering, you may take your sheet and see Mr. Jeffrey." Chrissy jumped up and was out the door before Mrs. Cooper could change her mind. "I want to remind each of you to pay attention to the clock and leave at your assigned time, no earlier. Is that clear?"

The entire class responded in unison. "Yes, Mrs. Cooper."

"Good. Now please open up your history books and begin answering the questions at the end of chapter seven."

All morning, students came and went from the classroom. Dale had difficulty concentrating on his schoolwork as each student returned and wrote an instrument on the board.

When Chrissy returned to class, she wrote *flute* by her name. As the list grew, it looked like this:

| | | | |
|---|---|---|---|
| Chrissy | Flute | Joe | Baritone |
| Victor | French horn | Gary | Alto saxophone |
| Tommy | Alto saxophone | Eugene | Trumpet |
| Dave | Percussion | Marie | French horn |
| Carol | Clarinet | Bobby | Clarinet |
| Francis | Trombone | Karl | Trombone |
| Sandra | Trumpet | | |

Dale felt his face getting flushed. He noticed that Eugene and Sandra had already selected trumpet. What if all the trumpet spots were filled before his time came? He chewed his nails as he walked down to the lunchroom.

As he slid beside Victor at the lunch table, Dale asked what happened at his meeting with Mr. Jeffrey.

"At first I was really nervous, but I relaxed when Mr. Jeffrey explained the process. He said French horn players need a good ear to hear the pitches, thin lips that turn down at the corners, and a mouth with little or no overbite." Victor straightened up in his seat. "He also said it helps to be tall enough to hold the instrument properly."

Victor continued. "Mr. Jeffrey played the piano and had me sing the pitches back. Then he asked me to make a buzzing sound on my lips like you do on the bugle." Victor demonstrated. "Finally, Mr. Jeffrey looked at my left hand and fingers. He said I had great lips for French horn and a really good ear for hearing and matching pitch. When he let me try the French horn, it took me a couple of tries to get the buzz right, but once I got the buzz going, I sounded really good."

Tommy said, "I didn't get tenor saxophone like I wanted because my hands and fingers are too small. Mr. Jeffrey said I would have trouble with my left hand hitting the palm keys since the tenor sax is bigger than the alto. I had no problem playing the alto. He sure knows his stuff."

Chrissy said, "I can't play tuba because my lips are too thin and the space between my top lip and nose is too small." Chrissy frowned and then burst into a big smile. "But Mr. Jeffrey said my top lip is perfect for flute since it has a slight frown to it... plus my fingers are long and not double jointed, which makes playing flute or clarinet harder. He asked me to pretend that I was pouting while I blew on the head joint. I did it, and what a sound I got! I can't wait until the first real lesson."

Victor said, "Now when you pout, you can just say you're practicing!" and he ducked as Chrissy playfully swung at her friend.

The rest of the table laughed and continued to share why they were selected for their particular instrument. Dale thought longingly about his appointment that was still over two hours away.

P. J. said, "I didn't get trombone, since Karl and Frances got it first, so I decided to take tuba." He puffed out his chest, "Mr. Jeffrey said I had great lungs and nice full lips, so either baritone or tuba would work." P. J. took a big bite of his bologna sandwich, chewing while he talked. "I like tuba because I only have to carry the mouthpiece and book home. I get one tuba here at school and the other tuba to keep at home... not a bad deal huh?"

Dale began to sweat upon hearing that some of the sections were full and students had to play other instruments that fit them just as well. He tried to rationalize that if he had to, he could play the French horn or baritone, since they both use mouthpieces. But in the end, he knew that there was no instrument other than the cornet that he truly wanted to play.

After lunch the gang went outside and played baseball, which helped take Dale's mind off of his meeting with Mr. Jeffrey. When the bell rang at the end of the lunch hour, it was only one o'clock. Mrs. Cooper always had thirty minutes of silent reading after lunch. Dale could hear the clock ticking on the wall. At one-fifteen, Nancy returned and wrote *percussion* by her name on the board, followed by

Rebecca     Oboe
Bridget     Alto saxophone

As Bridget walked by Dale's desk, she leaned down and said, "You're next. Good luck! I know you'll get cornet." She lightly brushed his hand.

Dale looked up into her bright blue eyes and mouthed the word "Thanks."

At two o'clock sharp, Dale went to the cloakroom and got his cornet out of his knapsack. His hands felt slippery on the handle of the case. As he walked, he could hear his shoes echo on the polished wood of the floor. When he got to the auditorium, he peered through the small panes of glass in the door. He could see Mr. Jeffrey sitting at a desk on the stage with a music stand next to him. Tables of instruments lined the edge of the stage. Dale took a deep breath and opened the auditorium door.

Mr. Jeffrey turned his head at the sound of the creaking door. "I've waited all day for you. Are you finally ready to begin?"

Dale swallowed. "I brought my cornet, if that's OK with you. I really want to play cornet."

"Why do you think I put you last?" He turned back to the desk and pulled out a cornet like Dale's. "I thought we would bypass the instrument selection process and have our first lesson today. I know how long you've waited, so I put you last so we could spend the rest of the school day learning how to play your new cornet. I even brought my own cornet so that we could play together. Let's get started."

Dale hurried down the aisle and hopped up the stairs onto the stage. He sat next to Mr. Jeffrey, placing the cornet case on the floor in front of him. "Can I ask you why everyone signed up for trumpet, and I'm going to play cornet?"

"Originally bands used cornets for their softer, mellower sound. Trumpets, which are longer, have a brighter sound that is used in orchestras. Because band students sometimes play in orchestras, it's cheaper to buy just a trumpet rather than buy both a cornet and a trumpet. There's no difference in the fingerings, only the brightness of the tone. We'll use both, and maybe when you get older and want to play in an orchestra, you can purchase a trumpet."

Mr. Jeffrey reached for books on the desk. "I have two books for you. The first one is the beginning method book everyone will use this year, the *Belwin Elementary Band Method*. The second book is one that all great players use, the *Arban's Complete Conservatory Method for Trumpet/Cornet*."

Dale examined the thick book. "Isn't the editor, Edwin Franko Goldwin, the conductor of the band at the ceremony where I got my new cornet?"

"You're right. He's not only a great conductor, he's also a composer, a cornet soloist, and he was my teacher when I learned to play."

Dale looked at his teacher admiringly. "Wow, you must be good, then."

"Pretty good, but I'm a better teacher than player, so let's get started."

Mr. Jeffrey handed him the Arban's book. Dale opened it and flipped through the pages as his teacher explained that the book had different sections and that a student plays parts of each section.

"It's a book with technical exercises, like lip slurs and long tones in addition to duets, famous cornet solos, and orchestra excerpts in the back."

Dale looked up. "What's an excerpt?"

"Excerpts are short melodies from famous orchestra pieces that all players should be able to play if they want to be great." Dale set the book back on the music stand. "I think you're going to be a great player. Let's see what you learned from playing the bugle."

Dale pulled the mouthpiece out of the case and buzzed long tones on his lips followed by buzzing the mouthpiece.

Next Dale repeated the same notes, but did lip slurs on the mouthpiece.

Mr. Jeffrey showed Dale how to hold the cornet with his left hand and put his right hand on the valves. Dale had never used valves before, and he liked the feel of the smooth pearl buttons as he pushed them up and down.

"Do you remember the notes you learned on the bugle?"

Dale nodded and said, "Low C below the staff, then G, C, and E in the staff, and high G above the staff. Do you want me to show you?"

Dale played each of the notes for Mr. Jeffrey, making sure to hold them out with a warm, round sound.

Mr. Jeffrey tapped his pencil on the stand. "You have a really good sound and a great range for a young player. Your grandfather did a fine job teaching you. Do you notice the big space between the low C below the staff and the first note on the staff G?"

"Yes, Grandpa told me that bugles can only play the open notes on the cornet or the ones that don't use valves. The notes in-between the open bugle notes need valves. Are we going to learn those now?

"Absolutely. Look at page three in the Belwin book and you'll see all the notes in-between and the fingers or the valves used to play them. Let's start with E on the staff."

12

Mr. Jeffrey said, "Always start on low C and work up to the E. Let me show you." Dale leaned forward as Mr. Jeffrey played a clear low C on his cornet and then put the first two valves down and played an E. "Now you try."

0          12

It took several tries, but Dale finally produced a solid low C.

"Good job! Now push your first two fingers down on the values and play an E."

Dale did as asked and out came an E. He took the cornet away from his lips. "I like using the valves."

"Just remember to keep your fingertips on the tops of the valves and keep your fingers curved. Don't play flat-fingered like this." Mr. Jeffrey put his fingers flat on the valves to demonstrate what not to do.

For the rest of the lesson, Dale learned all of the notes he'd not been able to play on the bugle. He learned the fingerings for D, E, F, A, and B-natural.

After reviewing the fingerings, Mr. Jeffrey said, "Let's finish up by playing your first scale, the C major scale. If you look on page eight, you'll see the scale written out for you. Can you tell me what all the music symbols mean?"

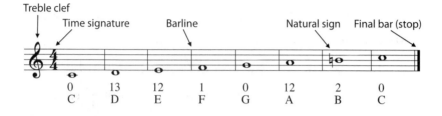

"That's easy. I learned all the symbols from Mrs. Vincent and my grandfather. The time signature means four beats a measure, and the quarter note gets one beat. The symbol next to it is a treble clef sign, and cornets are treble clef instruments. The big notes with no stem are whole notes. You hold them out for four counts, kind of like long tones. The small lines are barlines and show you how each measure is separated from the others, and the thin-and-thick pair of lines at the end means you are done. Oh, and I almost forgot, the symbol next to the B is a natural sign."

Mr. Jeffrey nodded. "I hope all my students are as smart as you. If so, we'll have a great band in no time. Let's play the scale together."

Dale and Mr. Jeffrey played up and down the scale. Dale forgot only a few of the fingerings, but after several tries, he was able to play the entire scale smoothly.

Mr. Jeffrey picked up his pencil. "I'm going to mark several exercises and pages in both books for you to work on before our next lesson and the first band practice next week. Now put the cornet away and let's get you back to class before the bell rings."

Dale gently put his cornet back in the case. Standing up, he stuck out his hand to shake Mr. Jeffrey's. Dale's dad had said that shaking another man's hand was a sign of respect.

"I'm looking forward to our next lesson."

Dale hurried back to class just in time to write *cornet* on the board in big letters next to his name.

As Dale turned, the entire class clapped, including Mrs. Cooper. The bell rang and the students pushed their chairs under their desks and filed out. Once outside, Dale and his friends met at the bike rack and rode to the fire station, where P. J. had promised everyone a cold cola from the machine in the firehouse. Smokey and Scout were up and ready as the boys pulled in, and Mr. Walsh, P. J.'s father, came out to greet them.

"From the all the noise you're making, you must be

excited about selecting your instruments. I want to hear what each one of you picked."

For the next hour and a half, the boys sat on the benches at the station talking with Mr. Walsh. They were startled to hear the five o'clock whistle from the Conn factory. Mr. Walsh stood up.

"See you tomorrow. I'm sure you'll have a lot to tell your parents at dinner tonight."

Dale hopped on his bike and pedaled home as fast as he could, Scout racing beside him. He skidded to a stop outside his house just as Grandma came out onto the porch, wiping her hands on her apron.

"Whoa! You must be in a hurry because you're hungry. I've made spaghetti and meatballs. Go wash your hands, we're ready to eat."

Grandpa was already seated as Dale slid into the chair. "What's this note on my plate?"

"Your mom left it for you because she had to go back to work tonight. Go on, read it."

Dale opened the note and read out loud.

Dale,

I called Captain Stonemiller about Scout joining the Dogs for Defense program. He said they still need dogs and would come by this Saturday at 9 a.m. to test him. Congratulations! I'll see you at breakfast to hear about band.

Love, Mom

Grandpa smiled. "Your dad would be proud of you for volunteering Scout. Now pass the noodles and tell me all about your day."

Chapter 5

# A TEST OF WILLS

Saturday mornings were always quiet in Libertyville. Dale liked to sit with Scout on the front porch in Grandpa's big wooden rocker before going off for a day of fun with the gang.

He couldn't believe how fast the week had gone since his first lesson. Each day, a different group of students had their first lesson with Mr. Jeffrey. Tuesday was woodwinds: flutes, clarinets, oboes, bassoons, and saxophones; Wednesday was low brass: baritones, trombones, and tubas; Thursday was high brass: trumpets, cornets, and French horns; and Friday was percussion. By the end of the week, all of the students had had one lesson and been given an assignment for the first full band rehearsal the next week.

The race after school on Friday had been one of the best, because Sandra asked if she could run. Dale liked Sandra, who was tall and slender, with long brown hair, and had the most amazing gray eyes he had ever seen. She had a wide smile and walked with her shoulders pulled back as if she owned the world. After school, she asked Dale if she could join them for the weekly race, since she was going to be playing trumpet and sitting right next to him. Dale knew she was smart and very competitive, and would challenge him at the cornet to see who was better.

Sandra won the race that day, much to the embarrassment of the boys, who said she was just lucky and dared her to come back next week.

Dale's thoughts were interrupted by the sound of a flute drifting out of Chrissy's window across the street. As he looked up, Chrissy stuck her head out the window and yelled, "What do you think of that?"

"It sounds great—play another one."

"I can't play another one. I only know one song. I'm going to work on my scales and arpeggios now. Oh, and good luck to Scout on his big test this morning."

Before Dale could answer, Chrissy ducked her head back inside and started playing again. The front door opened, and Dale's mother came out and sat down.

"Is it nine o'clock yet?" Dale said.

"Just fifteen minutes away."

Scout lay contently on the porch at Dale's feet. The dog had no idea that in a few minutes he would have to be on his best behavior. If Scout passed this initial test, he would be accepted in the official Dogs for Defense program. Although the qualifications weren't too stringent, the dogs that were accepted did have to have a certain degree of intelligence.

Scout's ears perked and he jumped up and stood alertly at the edge of the porch. "What is it, boy? What do you see?"

Just then, an olive green Army jeep appeared at the top of Simpson Hill. It hesitated a moment before turning into the Kingston driveway and jerking to a halt. Dale commanded, "Sit, Scout, sit" as a tall, wiry man wearing a dark green shirt and tie approached. Dale and his mom stood up as he reached the porch steps.

"Hello, son, I'm Captain Stonemiller," he said as he extended his hand to Dale. He then turned toward Dale's mother and saluted. "You must be Lieutenant Kingston."

"Yes, and this is my son, Dale, and his dog, Scout."

Captain Stonemiller looked at Scout carefully while he tapped a brightly shined shoe and shifted the clipboard that was tucked under his arm.

"I'll leave you two alone. If you need me, I'll be inside," Mom said as she turned and opened the front door.

Captain Stonemiller looked down at his clipboard and then knelt down next to Scout. "I don't recognize this breed of dog. What kind is he?"

"He's a Border Collie, sir. I gave him a haircut myself so he'd be ready for the Army."

Captain Stonemiller half-smiled, uncapped his fountain pen, and wrote a few quick notes on his forms.

"Let me tell you a little bit about Dogs for Defense." The Captain sat down in Grandpa's rocker while Dale climbed onto the porch swing.

"Dogs for Defense has always been an important part of the military. Throughout history, dogs have been used to help people defend themselves, their families, and their countries."

Captain Stonemiller moved to the edge of his chair and explained the openings available for guard, attack, and messenger dogs. "If Scout is accepted and trained to be a guard or attack dog, he won't be returned to you after the war ends. Dogs trained for these jobs learn to be loyal to one master and are dangerous to other people. These dogs can never return to being family pets."

Dale squirmed and reached down to stroke Scout, who was resting quietly at his feet.

"However, dogs used for messenger services will be returned to the family as soon as the war ends."

Dale felt his muscles start to relax.

"Which line of duty would you like to sign Scout up for?"

"Messenger dog." Dale knew in his heart that he could not bear to part with Scout forever. He glanced down at Scout, who looked up and seemed to nod his head in agreement.

"Scout looks like a fine, strong animal—just the kind of canine we're looking for." The captain crouched beside Scout, who looked up at him warily. With a practiced hand, he felt Scout's wet nose and then inspected the dog's teeth and gums. Next, he lifted Scout's ears and picked up each paw. Moving behind Scout, he checked the animal's hips and spine for alignment.

Writing some notes on his clipboard, he said, "Scout seems to be a very good-natured Border Collie. That's another trait we look for before we accept dogs into the program. High-strung or nervous dogs don't work well under the stressful conditions of war."

Dale's thoughts returned to the scene from the newsreel in which the dog was dodging enemy fire.

Captain Stonemiller was right, he thought. Dogs have to be cool and calm during battles.

"Let's take Scout to the backyard and see how he does on some tests for intelligence and obedience." Captain Stonemiller turned and walked briskly to the jeep to get his briefcase. Scout followed immediately, this time with Dale on *his* heels. Dale marveled at his dog's natural ability to understand people and situations.

Eager to show off his dog's intelligence, Dale ordered Scout to take the Captain to the backyard. Scout barked a response and took off at a jog toward the back yard. Captain Stonemiller nodded his head in approval.

"I can tell that Scout is well behaved by the way he follows your instructions. Now let's see how he does when *I* give him commands." Captain Stonemiller set his briefcase down on the grass in the backyard. Facing Scout, he commanded the dog to sit. Without hesitation Scout plunked his rear end down on the grass. Then Captain Stonemiller took a cloth ball out of his briefcase and let Scout take a sniff before throwing it toward the back of the yard.

"Fetch."

Thinking this was a great game, Scout reacted immediately, running to the ball and grabbing it with his teeth. Dale held his breath now. When he played with Scout, he always wanted Dale to chase him. Sure enough, Scout pranced around the back of the yard, waving the ball in his teeth and daring Captain Stonemiller to come and get it.

"Retrieve." Captain Stonemiller said, but Scout was having too good a time now running at the Captain, coming just within reach before swooping away in another direction.

Captain Stonemiller picked up the clipboard and began to write. Dale shoved his hands in his pockets as he shifted from foot to foot.

Tiring of the game, Scout trotted up to the Captain and offered him the ball. The Captain reached to pull the ball out of the dog's mouth, but the wily animal pulled back, growling and shaking his head in this game of tug of war. Unlike his master, who always loved playing this game, Captain Stonemiller let go of the ball, sending Scout staggering backwards a few steps. The dog then took off for a new round of laps around the backyard.

The captain jotted a few more notes on the form, placed his clipboard inside his briefcase, and snapped it shut. As he shook Dale's hand, he promised he would let Dale know whether or not Scout was accepted into the program within two weeks. He explained that he had five other dogs to interview that day, then turned and headed to his jeep. Dale ran after him, asking if he wanted to wait for Scout to return the ball to him.

Captain Stonemiller shook his head before climbing into the jeep and roaring out of the driveway.

Dale watched the jeep bounce toward the top of the hill while he dejectedly kicked a small stone. He felt a soft nudge on his hand and looked down at Scout who had placed the ball at Dale's feet.

"Why couldn't you have done that for Captain Stonemiller?"

He knelt down only to have the dog lick his face.

Dale shrugged his shoulders and then gathered his dog in his arms. "All we can do now is wait for Captain Stonemiller's call. Let's go meet the gang at the Jungle and forget all of this testing stuff."

Scout barked twice in reply.

Chapter 6

# WEEKS PASS

It had been two weeks since Captain Stonemiller's visit, and Dale had heard nothing. During that time, each student had four lessons. Finally the first day they would play as a band arrived. As Dale rode to school with his cornet in his knapsack that brisk November day, his mind was full of thoughts about Scout and the Dogs for Defense program. Then he felt his right hand tapping out the fingerings of a scale as he mouthed the names of the notes. It was good to have band to take his mind off of Captain Stonemiller. Now that the weather was turning colder, Scout stayed at home during school days, curled up under the porch in a warm hole he had dug next to the house's foundation.

Dale rounded the corner to see P. J. He held up his tuba mouthpiece and saluted as Dale slid to a stop.

"Let me get Smokey inside the fire station. He likes to climb into the trucks and sleep on the seats."

Dale pulled up the collar of his jacket as P. J. shooed Smokey into the building. "I think winter is coming. From the look of those clouds, we may even have snow in a few weeks."

"I hope you're right. I'm ready for some serious snowball fights and sledding on that toboggan you want for Christmas."

Dale and P. J. took off out of the driveway. "Since it's getting so cold, let's make today's race with the girls our last until spring."

P. J. struggled to keep up with Dale. "I'm tired of the girls winning and Victor whining about losing."

By the time the boys got to school, the others were at the bike rack, unloading their instruments.

Tommy grabbed his alto sax. "Come on, you slowpokes! Let's get inside, I'm freezing."

The bell rang, and the boys crowded through the doors of Emerson School. As Dale made his way through the narrow hallway, he realized he was walking next to Bridget, Chrissy, and Sandra, who were also carrying their instruments. Bridget flashed her teeth in a wide smile when she saw Dale. "We've been talking. Maybe we should make today our last race."

"Would you believe that P. J. and I said the same thing earlier this morning?"

Chrissy nodded, "Then we're all in agreement that today is our last race."

Just then Victor pushed in-between Dale and the girls, knocking Dale's leg with his French horn case. "Good. I need some time off to get faster." He lugged his horn up the stairs, racing to beat everyone into Mrs. Cooper's room.

As they filed into the classroom, putting away their coats and instruments, Dave said, "I think we're having band first thing this morning."

Each day Mrs. Cooper would write the day's schedule on the board. At the top of the chalkboard was:

$$BAND\ 8{:}00 - 9{:}00$$

She had been shuffling through some papers on her desk, but now stood and greeted the class. "I'd like to review today's schedule." She walked over to the board. "Mr. Jeffrey will begin having band on Mondays,

Wednesdays, and Fridays, and group lessons on Tuesdays and Thursdays. From now on, band students will report directly to the auditorium on the days you have band, so you'll start your day there. That way you can warm up before rehearsal. Please get your instruments and go quietly to the auditorium. Mr. Jeffrey is waiting."

Mrs. Cooper had barely finished talking before everyone was up and out the door. Mr. Jeffery stood with his arms crossed at the entrance.

"Let's stop here. I want to explain how I'd like you to behave in the auditorium and when you take your seats onstage." P. J., who had been the last to leave the classroom, wiggled through the crowd so that he could stand next to Mr. Jeffrey. "First, I want to congratulate you on two great weeks of lessons. It takes lots of hard work to learn an instrument." He paused before continuing.

"Today we'll begin to build a great band. Band is a group experience, and that's what we'll focus our time and energy on. Every student will respect each other's right to a quality musical experience by following a few simple rules." P. J. nodded.

"First, you'll enter the auditorium quietly and set up the chairs onstage. You'll get your instruments out very carefully, then sit down so that you can warm up properly. Brass players will always buzz their lips, followed by buzzing the mouthpiece, then finally proceeding to long tones." Just then Victor made a loud *bzzzzzzzzzzz* and everyone laughed except Mr. Jeffrey, who frowned and said, "Victor, even though I'm not on the podium, I'll not allow any talking or misbehavior at any time, as it's a sign of disrespect to me and your fellow band members." Victor looked down at his shoes.

Mr. Jeffrey continued, "The woodwinds will start with long tones and then arpeggios." Chrissy held her flute case up to her mouth and pretended to play a scale up and down. Mr. Jeffrey said, "I'll start each rehearsal at exactly eight o'clock, so don't be late." Then he softened his tone and said. "I hope everyone is as excited as I am to get started. Let's begin making a great band."

P. J. was the first to go in, and he turned and echoed Mr. Jeffrey, "Yeah, let's go make a great band," and everybody cheered as they entered the auditorium to begin their first rehearsal.

Once they got to the stage, Sandra put her trumpet case down and put her finger to her mouth. "Shh… remember what Mr. Jeffrey said about being quiet." They silently put their instruments together. The chairs were already set up in half circles, and nametags marking where they should sit were on each chair. The sounds of buzzing, long tones, and arpeggios began to fill the air. Dale sat back in his chair after playing his warm-up and looked proudly at each of his friends. He had dreamed of this moment ever since Mr. Greenleaf had presented him with his cornet.

Finally Mr. Jeffrey stepped on the podium, and the playing stopped. "Open your books to page four, exercise one."

Mr. Jeffrey explained that the first few exercises were in unison, which meant that everyone played the same pitch. He lifted his arms and said, "One, two, ready, play...." As they played the first note, Sandra turned and looked at Victor, who was sitting behind her. He kept trying to hit the right note, and on the third try, he finally got it. P. J. turned bright red as a low note rumbled out of his tuba, while Bobby made a loud squeak on his clarinet. Karl kept adjusting the slide of his trombone until his note matched the others. After playing the exercise several times, Mr. Jeffrey put his arms down and said, "This next exercise will sound more like real band music. This song has harmony, or different pitches played by different instruments all at the same time."

P. J. blurted out, "Do you mean real music? A real song?"

"Yes, P. J., a real song. Turn to page eleven and let's play "Lightly Row," which everyone should have practiced."

For the rest of the rehearsal they worked on the song as a group. Then Mr. Jeffrey said, "Now I'm going to ask someone to play the song alone. Before anyone volunteers, remember that a musician's efforts should be respected. Please be quiet while the person plays and then clap at the end. Do I have a volunteer to go first?"

Everyone sat quietly and looked at one another until Sandra raised her hand. "I'll play it."

"OK… whenever you're ready."

Sandra licked her lips, took a deep breath, and brought her trumpet up to her lips. She played the first note to make sure she had the right pitch.

With the horn still up to her lips, Sandra silently practiced the fingerings of the song as Mr. Jeffrey shifted his feet on the podium. Dale, who was sitting next to Sandra, leaned over, "Just pretend you're at home in your room all by yourself."

Sandra nodded and began to play, softly at first, but then with more confidence.

Bridget followed her music and fingered the notes along with Sandra as she played the song straight through. When she finished the last note, everyone applauded. Victor's hand shot up next, and one by one, all the members of the band slowly struggled through the song before Mr. Jeffrey said, "Let's end today's rehearsal by playing "Lightly Row" one more time as a group."

At the end of the rehearsal, Mr. Jeffrey asked everyone to put their instruments away carefully and move the chairs and the stands to the side of the stage.

"Thanks for a great rehearsal! Enjoy your weekend. And Victor, I want to hear on Monday who won the last race after school today."

"How'd you know about the race?"

"That's all you've been talking about this morning."

Tommy rushed over and set his alto sax case on Victor's toe. Victor hopped back, as Tommy said, "The only way Victor will win is if he runs by himself!"

Mr. Jeffrey turned to pick up his score. "Enough of the race talk. Now please go quietly back to Mrs. Cooper's class."

Dale walked back to class next to Sandra. "I thought you played great today."

Sandra looked into Dale's brown eyes. "Thanks! It's fun sitting next to you. I'm looking forward to getting to know you better and playing our horns together."

Before Dale could answer, Sandra turned and began talking to Bridget. Dale felt a jab in his back and spun around.

In a high voice, Karl said, "Aren't you going to tell me how good I played?" and he batted his eyelashes at P. J., who was walking with him.

Dale turned red and shook his head as they entered the classroom. The rest of the day flew by, and before Dale knew it, the final bell rang. The gang headed to the track for the last race of the season. P. J. led the way, followed by Chrissy, Bridget, Sandra, Victor, Karl, Bobby, Dave, and Tommy. When they reached the track, they set their books and instruments down to warm up for the race. Victor jogged slowly up and down the lanes while the girls stretched from side to side in anticipation of their victory.

After a few minutes, P. J. announced in his best imitation of the gravelly voice of their gym teacher, Mr. Cabutti, "Let's settle down and get into position." P. J. looked around. "Hey, where's Tony? He's always the line judge. Who's going to do that?"

Bridget walked up to P. J. "He's not coming, but you can start us and watch the finish line." She winked at P. J. "I've got a feeling you'll be able to see who wins easily today."

P. J. ran down to the finish line, turned and mopped the sweat that was forming on his brow in the cool November air. "Don't cheat and jump off early," he warned as the gang took their places at the start.

Dale turned to Victor and advised, "I think you should run on the far right lane today. That's the fastest lane.

Maybe you can win if you keep your head down and focus on the finish line."

Victor nodded. Dale said, "Don't look back; it's the only way to win." They got down into position.

"On your mark, get set, go," P. J. shouted.

Victor took off, his head down, focusing on the track in front of him. He could hear the crunch of cinders as his legs pumped up and down in rhythm. He glanced up and saw P. J. cheering and jumping up and down at the finish line. He lowered his head and repeated Dale's advice, "Don't look back... don't look back." Streaking across the finish line, he heard P. J. announce, "And the winner is... Victor!"

Victor slowed to a stop and pumped his arms in the air. "I won, I won!" As he turned around to see who was next to cross the finish line, he could see the gang still standing at the starting line, laughing. Victor looked at P. J. who was doubled over laughing. "Didn't I win?" he said as Dale and the gang jogged up. Karl patted Victor on the back. "After hearing you whine about not winning all week, and this being the last race until spring, we thought we'd let you win. That way we don't have to hear you whine for the next four months."

Victor stood speechless, his mouth wide open. Finally he said, "That was a pretty good joke." Then he straightened up. "I really did win, didn't I? After all, a win is a win."

The group walked back to the side of the track where they had put their books and instruments. P. J. turned to Chrissy, "How come you never let me win like you did Victor?"

Chrissy smiled and put her arm around him. "Because we like you."

P. J. blushed, "You do?"

Everyone laughed and headed off for home.

After leaving P. J. at the firehouse, Dale rode especially fast up Simpson Hill. He gave a loud whistle when he reached the top, and Scout shot out from under the porch. He slid his bike to a stop, hopped off just as Scout jumped in his arms and licked his face.

"Let's go inside and get warm." Just then, his mother opened the front door and stood on the porch with a piece of paper in her hand.

Dale bounded up the front steps with Scout close behind him. She handed a letter to Dale. "I think it's from Captain Stonemiller."

Grandma was working at the counter, preparing dinner as Dale sat down at the table. He looked at the official envelope with *The Department of the Army* written on the top. Before he opened it, he reached down and patted Scout on the head. "Either way, if you make it or not, you're a great dog." Slowly, Dale opened the envelope and read the letter aloud:

```
To: Dale Kingston


    It is my honor and duty to inform you that
your dog, Scout Kingston, has been accepted
into the Dogs for Defense Program. Scout will
be assigned to the messenger program.
    Scout is to report to the Libertyville train
station at 1100 hours this Sunday, November
19, 1944. Scout will be transported to Fort
Robinson, Nebraska, where he will undergo his
training before being shipped overseas to serve
his country in the war.
    Congratulations on Scout's appointment to
Dogs for Defense — messenger division.


                        Captain Stonemiller
```

Dale set the letter down and sat in silence. He could hear Grandma chopping carrots on the cutting board. He thought, "Have I really signed Scout up to go to war and leave me forever?" Scenes from the newsreel with a dog dodging enemy fire flashed through Dale's mind.

His mother put her arms around him as his eyes filled with tears. "Remember, a dog like Scout saved your Dad's life," and she gave him a hug. "You're doing a brave thing. Your father would be proud of you. In fact, we're all proud of you."

Dale hugged his mom and then leaned down to scratch Scout behind the ears. His dog looked up at Dale and tilted his head. "At least I have two days to play with you before you go." Dale stood up, "Come on, let's play." And Dale and Scout raced out the back door.

Chapter 7

# SAYING GOODBYE

Dale woke up on Sunday morning to the smell of freshly brewed coffee, sausages, and pancakes. He snuggled next to Scout, who had been allowed to sleep on his bed the last two nights before his departure to Fort Robinson.

"No church today," Dale said rubbing Scout's head. "We have to be at the train station at eleven hundred hours." Dale laid his head on Scout's soft fur and thought about yesterday and all they had done together since finding out Scout would be leaving.

The last trip to the Jungle with the gang and the last game of Capture the Flag had been one of the best ever. Even Victor had tears in his eyes when he hugged Scout and said, "You stay safe and come back to us as soon as the war is over." Scout seemed to understand and barked twice in reply. Before the gang got on their bikes, P. J. knelt and shook Scout's paw, solemnly wishing him luck. Even Smokey sensed something was happening and licked Scout's nose and rubbed against his side before he took off after P. J.

When Dale and Scout arrived home, Chrissy and Bridget were sitting on his front porch. Scout ran up to the girls and rolled on his back, a sign that he wanted a belly scratch. While Bridget leaned over to scratch him, Chrissy pulled a green camouflage-colored handkerchief from her purse.

"We made a gift for Scout and wanted to give it to him before he goes to Fort Robinson. We thought he could wear this bandana," Chrissy said as she unfurled the scarf and tied it around Scout's neck.

Scout sat patiently while Chrissy adjusted the scarf. She gave Scout a hug, and the dog licked her ear in return. "You're one special dog." Bridget added, "You're so brave to send him off to serve his country. I don't think I could do that with my dog."

Dale straightened up. "I'm going to miss him, but if

he can save someone's life, then it's worth it."

The girls bent down and gave Scout a final pat. "You be safe and come back to us soon." Scout barked twice in reply.

"Come on, Bridget. Let's go before I cry," Chrissy said, and the two girls left to go back to Chrissy's house.

Dale's thoughts returned to the present, and he snuggled closer to Scout in bed and stroked his fur.

"Come on, Scout. Let's get some breakfast."

Scout leapt off the bed and scampered down the steps to the kitchen. Dale followed and slid into his chair next to Grandpa. His mother poured him a glass of orange juice. "Did Scout enjoy sleeping in your bed last night?"

"He even put his head on my pillow. But he sure does have dog breath."

Grandpa laughed. "I'm sure he does after the bones Grandma gave him yesterday." Grandma, who was flipping pancakes at the stove, ignored the comment. "Did you finish packing?"

"I packed a knapsack with his favorite things—his ball and his pillow. I also wrote a note to the handlers at Fort Robinson. Can I read it to you?"

"Sure… I'll pour you a cup of coffee while you get it."

Dale ran up the stairs to his room. By the time he got back, a steaming cup of coffee with cream was at his place. Grandma dried her hands and sat down at the table next to Grandpa while Mother leaned against the counter. Dale lightly blew on the coffee and took a sip. He then unfolded the note and began to read.

---

To Whom It May Concern:

This is my dog Scout. I'm sure he will make a good soldier and messenger dog. I don't want him to feel homesick, so I'm sending some of his favorite things. If he gets lonely at night, just give him this pillow and scratch him behind his ears until he falls asleep. His favorite game is catch. I have packed his ball for him to play with if he has some free time. Please take good care of my dog. I love him very much.

Sincerely,
Dale Kingston

P.S. Be careful when you give Scout a bath. He hates them.

Dale folded the note and inserted it in the knapsack. His mother stepped behind Dale's chair and put her hands on his shoulders.

"Dale, the handlers will be able to see that you love your dog and will take great care of Scout."

Grandma stood up and took a heaping plate of pancakes out of the oven where they had been warming. "Let's eat breakfast. We don't want to be late for the train."

Dale had a few bites of pancake and sausage, but he didn't seem hungry. "May I be excused to get dressed?" Mother looked at Grandma, who was about to say No before Grandpa jumped in. "Sure, boy, do what you need to do."

Fifteen minutes later Dale walked into the living room where the family was waiting. Scout tilted his head at the tinkling of his leash and whimpered. Dale took a deep breath and hooked the worn leash to the dog's collar. He glanced at Grandpa, who had put on his Sunday coat and hat, and ordered Scout to heel as he walked him down the steps of the front porch for the last time.

Scout tugged on the leash, begging for one last dash around the yard. Mother and Grandma stood waving on the porch. Not wanting to prolong the departure,

Grandpa opened the car door, knowing that Scout loved going for car rides and hanging his head out the window. The dog hesitated before finally jumping in.

Ever since the war began, the family took fewer and fewer outings in the automobile. Petroleum was needed by the armed forces to fuel planes, tanks, and ships, so gasoline for everyday use was becoming more and more scarce. Trips by car were now reserved only for special occasions.

As the car navigated through the maze of streets, Dale sat quietly in the back seat. He laid his head against the dog's familiar fur. The rhythmic beating of Scout's heart comforted him. He tried not to think about what soon was going to happen when they arrived at the train station.

The train station was bustling with activity. Soldiers were hugging girlfriends, families were saying their goodbyes to sons and brothers, and luggage handlers were moving great pyramids of luggage on carts. Scout pulled at his leash as Dale followed Grandpa past the station to a gated area on the west side of the railroad yard. While they walked along, Scout's nose swept the ground as he sniffed to detect a recognizable scent in the foreign territory. Dale glanced at Grandpa's watch as he opened the gate to the enclosure—eleven hundred hours sharp.

The creaking gate alerted Captain Stonemiller, who popped up from behind a stack of wooden crates. He strode over to Dale and Grandpa, shook their hands, and said, "Right on time. Excellent! We'll put Scout in this crate to be shipped on the next train, which should be arriving in about fifteen minutes." The captain patted the large crate next to him.

Dale stroked Scout's tufted black-and-white fur, "Sir, I've packed this knapsack for Scout to take to Fort Robinson. Can I put it in his crate?"

Captain Stonemiller glanced down at Dale's serious brown eyes. "I guess it wouldn't hurt anything." Dale placed the knapsack in the bottom of the wooden crate and stood holding his dog's leash as he gazed into the empty crate. Captain Stonemiller gently patted Dale's shoulders.

Resuming his businesslike manner, the captain asked Dale for the leash, which he tied securely to the fence. No longer able to contain the flood of tears, Dale turned and buried his head in his grandfather's coat. Grandpa knelt and looked directly into Dale's eyes.

"This is a very brave thing you're doing for your country, son. You're making the biggest sacrifice any boy can make by volunteering Scout."

Breaking free from his grandfather, Dale ran to Scout and gave him one last, deep hug. He whispered, "Do your best, Scout. I love you." Dale felt his courage ebbing away, so he quickly turned and dashed to the gate. He opened it and ran blurry-eyed past the station, holding his hands over his ears, trying to block out Scout's piercing bark. As he ran toward the car, he could still hear the dog's unending staccato yip, which seemed to be Morse code for help.

Finally Dale reached the car, where he fell into the backseat, burying his head in his arms. Fifteen minutes later, he heard the car door open and Grandpa slide into the front seat. He sat quietly before starting the engine. Just then, a loud whistle could be heard, signaling a train was leaving the station. Scout was beginning his journey to Fort Robinson.

Chapter 8

# FORT ROBINSON

The five crates containing Scout and the other dogs were carefully lifted off the train and loaded onto the dusty green army truck for delivery to Fort Robinson. The dogs, sensing a change, pawed the sides of their crates and whimpered.

"Settle down, boys," Private Artie Klimza said, the one assigned the task of picking up the dogs from the train station. Like the dogs, Artie was also new to Fort Robinson. He had been born and raised on a ranch in Montana. After graduation from high school, he signed up for the Army. His background of living on a ranch and his love of animals helped to get him assigned to the Canine Corps. Klimza swung his lanky body up into the driver's seat, started the engine, and took off for camp.

The truck wheeled up to the entry gate, and the sentry waved Artie through. He pulled up to the quarantine kennel where canine recruits were required to spend their first few nights. Isolating the dogs prevented the spread of unwanted diseases and allowed them to become accustomed to their new surroundings.

Scout scratched at the sides of his crate. He had been cooped up for two days on the train, and longed to be free. Artie lifted the crates off the truck. Carefully he pried off the top, unsure as to what kind of reception he would get. When he opened a crate from the last shipment, a German shepherd nipped him on the finger as if it were Artie's fault that the dog had had a long, rough ride. One by one, he led the dogs to individual kennels, where the camp veterinarian quickly inspected each animal for any injuries that might have occurred during the trip.

Scout's crate was the last to be opened. The dog stood as the lid was lifted, and the box was flooded with sunlight. Scout leapt up like a jack-in-the box, placing his paws on the side of the crate and holding the knapsack in his mouth.

Scout dropped the pack at Artie's feet. After snapping a leash on the dog's collar, Artie picked up the pack and placed it next to the empty crate.

"C'mon, boy. Let's run!" Artie said as he jogged down the grassy patch in front of the kennel. Grateful for his release and anxious for exercise, Scout pulled on the leash. After a few times up and down the path, Artie opened the gate to the kennel and led the dog inside, where he unhooked the leash. While Scout sniffed the new area and the vet inspected Scout for injuries, Artie went outside to shut the gate. He glanced at the empty crate and spied the dusty knapsack. He unsnapped the flap and pulled out a worn ball, a small pillow, and a note.

Artie smiled as he read the carefully printed instructions. He knew what it was like to be away from a pet for a long time. In the months since he had left Montana, Artie had thought daily about his own dog, Rusty, who was at home working on his family's sheep ranch. Although he had never met Dale Kingston, Artie felt a strong kinship with the boy who had laboriously and lovingly written this note. Artie refolded the letter along the original crease marks and slipped it in his back pocket.

After the vet finished, Artie gave Scout a dish of water, which the dog lapped up. The private stood at the fence, his arms overhead resting on the links.

"So your name is Scout. Hmmm... You sound like just the kind of dog I'd like to work with. I'll ask Sergeant Stafford tomorrow if I can be your handler."

Chapter 9

# HOLIDAYS APPROACH

As Dale came down to breakfast on Monday, he missed seeing Scout, but he was feeling a little better about his decision to volunteer his dog. He had written a letter to his dad in the South Pacific about Scout being selected for Dogs for Defense and having to take him to the train. Writing the letter helped Dale realize that other young boys had done the same thing. He set the letter on the kitchen table and sat down for breakfast.

"Mom, can you address this letter and take it to the post office today?"

"Sure. I even wrote one myself last night, so the two can go together."

Grandpa, who had been reading the paper, said, "I think with Thanksgiving, the Tommy Dorsey/Andrews Sisters Concert, and your first band concert, you'll be busy. That'll take your mind off of Scout and your dad."

Dale took a gulp of his orange juice. "I almost forgot about band this morning. I need to hurry so I can help set up the chairs and stands for Mr. Jeffrey."

"What time is band?" Grandma said.

"Eight o'clock sharp, and Mr. Jeffrey warned us about being late." Dale gobbled the rest of his oatmeal, scraping the sides of his bowl. He stood up and Grandma handed him his lunch. "Don't forget your hat and your instrument."

In a flash, Dale was out the door and riding down Simpson Hill. As he rounded the corner to the firehouse, P. J. was riding down the driveway. "Come on, let's hurry!" P. J. shouted as they pedaled toward school.

The two arrived at the bike rack just as Chrissy, Bridget, and Sandra were heading inside with their books and instruments. P. J. jumped off his bike. "I don't want to be last!"

Once inside the school, the boys ran to the auditorium. Just before they entered, Dale reminded P. J. to be quiet and help set up before they warmed up.

"I remember, I remember," P. J. said, flinging open the door to the auditorium.

Victor set a stand in front of a chair on the stage. "Look who the slowpokes are this time." Sandra set two more stands in front of chairs while Chrissy helped carry more to set out. "There's no way you were going to beat me here today." He set another chair down with a thud. "I'm going to run here every day as training for our next race in the spring. You're never going to have to let me win again."

Mr. Jeffrey came out from behind the curtain with his podium. "I heard about the race, and it sounds like it was a good practical joke, Victor. But enough of this race talk. Let's finish setting up so you can warm up."

Once the chairs and stands were arranged in semi-circles, everyone unpacked their instruments and began warming up. At exactly eight o'clock, Mr. Jeffrey stepped on the podium. Everyone knew that was the signal to stop playing and wait for instructions. "Please turn to page four, number one." The director reminded everyone to watch his baton and stay in tempo.

Dave, who was standing in the back with the percussion, set his mallets on the bells and raised his hand. "Why do we need to look at your baton?" Why do you swish it back and forth like that?"

Before Mr. Jeffrey could respond, P. J. made a swishing sound like a sword cutting through the air. Everyone laughed.

"Good question. But we can do without P. J.'s sound effects," he said as he set his baton on the stand. "Musicians watch the baton so that they can all keep the same tempo or beat. With thirty different students playing at once, by watching the baton, you can all stay together as you play. Can you imagine what it would sound like if we all played at different speeds?" Mr. Jeffrey picked up his baton to demonstrate. "I want everyone to turn to "Lightly Row." Put your instruments up, and when I say 'Go,' I want you to all play. I'm not going to conduct."

The students put their instruments up, and when Mr. Jeffrey said, "Go," they started playing. After a few seconds, thirty different versions of the song could be heard.

Mr. Jeffrey cut the group off. "Now let's do it again, but this time watch the baton for the beat." The band now played together as one player.

Dave raised his hand again. "That makes sense, but what about the swishing movement?"

Mr. Jeffrey held up his baton. "Let's make this simple. When my baton moves up the first time, that's called a pick-up beat. Then when it comes straight down, that is beat one." Mr. Jeffrey demonstrated by moving his baton up and then straight down. "Now, when the baton goes to the left that is beat two, and when it goes to the right that is beat three." Mr. Jeffrey moved his baton from side to side. "Finally, I move the baton back up to beat four. I then just keep repeating that movement until the song is finished." The director demonstrated each movement as he made the following pattern with his baton.

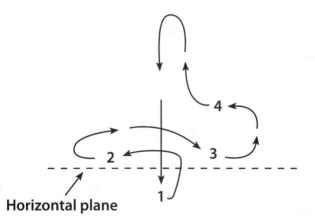

**Horizontal plane**

"Can we try to conduct the pattern to see how it feels?" Bridget said. Mr. Jeffrey smiled. "Learning to conduct the $\frac{4}{4}$ pattern will help you understand the importance of watching a conductor." As the band members followed his hand movements, Mr. Jeffrey said, "Remember: down, left, right, and then up."

After a few tries at the pattern Mr. Jeffrey stopped the group. "Wait a minute, Karl and Tommy, your other left. You're going the wrong way."

Everyone laughed, and Mr. Jeffrey held up his hand for silence. "Sorry, Mr. Jeffrey," Karl said, "but we were watching your arms. Since you're facing us, we moved the same direction as you."

"You're right. Let me turn around so we're facing the same direction."

This time everyone's arms went in the same direction. Gradually Mr. Jeffrey turned around, and Karl shouted out, "I got it, I got it."

The next thirty minutes were full of stopping, starting, working on tone, breathing in tempo, tonguing, and individual students playing their parts.

Finally Chrissy raised her hand. "How come Victor's French horn part and Bobby's clarinet part have different notes? Aren't we all playing the same pitch?"

"That's because not all instruments are C instruments, which means they sound like they are written in the music." Mr. Jeffrey asked the C instruments—flutes, oboes, bassoons, trombones, tubas, and mallets—to play the note C on page five, number seventeen. "I'll play the same note on the piano,"

Mr. Jeffrey played a concert C on the piano, and everyone played the same note. "That sounds the same," blurted P. J.

"Now let's hear the B-flat instruments. Do I have a volunteer from the cornets, trumpets, clarinets, tenor saxophones, or treble clef baritones? I'll play the same C on the piano while you play your C on your instruments."

Bobby played a C on his clarinet while Mr. Jeffrey played a C on the piano. Tommy groaned. "That sounds terrible!"

"Bobby played the correct note, but since his instrument is in B-flat, he has to play one note higher than the concert pitch to make it sound like the same note. Bobby, play your D, and I'll play the C again, and let's see what happens."

Bobby looked around. "Are you sure?" Mr. Jeffrey nodded.

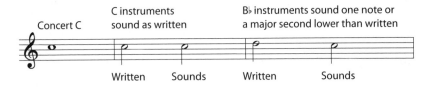

He put his clarinet to his lips and played a D as Mr. Jeffrey again played a C. This time they sounded the same. P. J. clapped from the back of the tuba section, and Bobby stood up and bowed.

Victor's hand shot up. "My music says it's in F. Are we different than the C and B-flat instruments?"

"Yes, French horns are in F and sound a perfect fourth higher than written. Remember when we learned what a perfect fourth sounds like in your lesson last week?

Victor said, "It begins the song 'Here Comes the Bride,'" and he sang out, "Here comes the bride, all fat and wide!"

Everyone laughed, and Mr. Jeffrey settled the group down by sternly asking Victor to play his G while he played concert C on the piano.

Victor tilted his head. "Aren't you going to have me sound bad and then change the note so I sound the same as you?"

"Not unless you don't play the G correctly."

F instruments sound a perfect
fourth higher than written

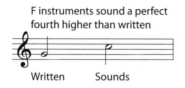

Written      Sounds

Victor played his G as Mr. Jeffrey played concert C on the piano, and the band clapped. Finally, Bridget raised her hand.

"Mr. Jeffrey, our sax music says it's in E-flat, so we must be different also. Is that right?"

"Yes, you sound three notes, or a minor third, higher than written. Bridget, play an A, and I'll play the same concert C." He glanced over at Victor, "And no, I'm not tricking you."

Bridget took a deep breath and played an A while Mr. Jeffrey played his concert C on the piano.

E♭ instruments sound a minor
third higher than written

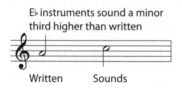

Written      Sounds

They sounded the same and everyone clapped.

"We're running out of time. Does everyone understand that all instruments are not in the same key?" Mr. Jeffrey pointed to the examples on the board.

Tommy said, "Why is that?"

Mr. Jeffrey set his baton on the stand. "Each instrument is made in the key that makes the instrument easier to manufacture and play in tune. It has a lot to do with acoustics, or sound. I'll explain further in each of your lessons." He picked up his baton and held up his hands. "Let's finish with page fourteen, number ninety-five, 'Rolling Along.'"

The band played straight through without any mistakes. Mr. Jeffrey smiled and said, "Since this Thursday is Thanksgiving, we won't have band or lessons until the following Monday. I have a folder on this table with all of the new music we'll perform at our first concert in four weeks. Please pick up one with your name on it and practice over the Thanksgiving holiday. Now let's put the chairs and stands away."

Everyone closed their music folders and put their instruments in their cases. P. J. grabbed two stands in each hand and raised them above his head like he was lifting weights. He turned to see Chrissy and Bridget chatting by their instrument cases, so he set the stands down and tiptoed up behind them. He started clapping and singing the Clean-Up Song that they had learned in kindergarten.

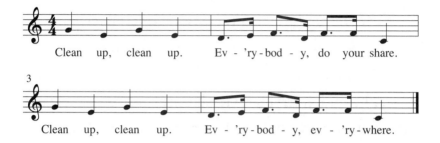

Clean up, clean up. Ev - 'ry - bod - y, do your share.

Clean up, clean up. Ev - 'ry - bod - y, ev - 'ry - where.

The girls turned and blushed as everyone joined P. J.'s singing. They quickly latched their cases, realizing they should be helping.

"I haven't heard that song in years," Chrissy said as she and Bridget grabbed their chairs and began singing along. They cleared the stage in no time.

Mr. Jeffrey said, "You're a better band than a choir, but at least singing got the job done. Now off to class!" Mr. Jeffrey turned and walked away humming "Clean up, clean up."

Mrs. Johnstone, who was wearing a white smock spattered with different colors of paint, was waiting for the class outside the art room. She greeted each student with a smile, making them feel special as they entered her room. "Dale, I heard the band playing this morning. You sounded great."

"Thanks," Dale said. "We're really working hard."

"I'm looking forward to your first concert," she said. As the last person entered the classroom, she closed the door. "If you get busy painting your papier-mâché turkey, you'll be able to take it home for the holidays."

Dale nodded. "It'll look great on the dining room table," he said, hurrying to get his art supplies. Dale liked Mrs. Johnstone's bright red hair and piercing blue eyes, but he was a little scared of her sharp, edgy voice.

The class flew by as everyone put the finishing touches on their papier-mâché projects. Some had made horns of plenty, while others had made turkeys. A few had made big rocks to depict Plymouth Rock. By the end of class Dale had brown, green, and red paint all over his face, clothes, and hair.

P. J., who was working at the table next to Dale, took his brush and said, "Let me add some marks to the slash of brown paint on your face. Then you'll look just like Boris Karloff in Frankenstein." P. J. raised his brush toward Dale's cheek.

Just then, Mrs. Johnstone's voice cut through the air like a knife. "P. J., enough of that. You have work to do!" The class laughed as P. J. lowered his head and turned back to his table. "Please be quiet. Dale, you're a mess, so wash up before lunch."

"Yes, ma'am," Dale said as he went back to work, adding details to his turkey.

Mrs. Johnston examined his work. "I think you can take it home today after it dries."

As the class drew to a close, everyone put the finishing touches on their projects, then cleaned up and put away the art supplies.

Victor, who had made a huge papier-mâché rock with the date 1620 painted on the side, pretended to be Hercules and mock struggled as he hoisted the rock over his head.

Mrs. Johnstone heard the grunting and turned, unleashing her teacher voice. "Victor, please put that rock down and finish cleaning up. I'm very disappointed in your behavior, but I'm more disappointed that you can hardly lift a five-pound paper rock. Maybe Mr. Cabutti will have to work you a little harder in gym class." Everyone laughed and started humming the Clean-Up Song.

Dale returned from washing up, and P. J. leaned over. "Your turkey is making me really hungry." Just then the bell signaling lunch rang. While getting their lunches from Mrs. Cooper's class, Karl, Dave, and Bobby made grunting sounds, pretending they were Victor, struggling with his papier-mâché rock.

Bridget poked Victor in the back. "If your peanut butter sandwiches and cookies are too heavy, I could carry them for you."

Victor laughed. "OK, you got me this time; but you have to admit it was kind of funny to lift a fake rock like it weighed a ton."

Tommy jumped in. "I thought of doing the same thing, but I'm glad you did it first so you got in trouble, not me."

After lunch, they learned more about the early-American pilgrims, and then took a math quiz and a spelling test. By the time it was three o'clock, Dale's head hurt from all of the thinking and test taking. As he packed up his books, Sandra came up to him.

"I hear you have tickets to the Tommy Dorsey/Andrews Sisters concert in two weeks. Do you think you can get one for me?"

Dale turned and looked into her gray eyes and said, "Let me see what I can do. I can't promise anything."

Sandra leaned closer, lightly brushing her hand on his.

"Thanks for trying! You're the best."

Dale blushed as the bell rang and she turned away.

P. J., who had been watching, brushed past him, saying, "Enough of this girl stuff. Let's get our art projects and figure out how we're going to ride home with our instruments, books, your turkey, and my rock."

The gang hurried to the art room, picked up their projects, and went to the bike rack. "I know I'm not supposed to ride with no hands, but I don't think I have a choice," Dale said as he got on his bike and tried to balance.

"I've got an idea. I'll take my belt off and make a sling out of it. The rock can hang from my shoulder." Before anyone could say anything, P. J. had his belt off and was tying it to the rock. With both arms in the air, his pants slipped off. He stood next to his bike with his belt on his shoulder, a rock hanging from it, and his pants down on his ankles.

For a few seconds, the boys just stared. Finally, they burst out laughing. Tommy spoke up.

"So much for that idea!"

P. J. quickly put the rock down, pulled up his pants and replaced the belt, while he looked around to make sure no girls were present. "OK, no hands it is." Then he said, "Please don't give me a new nickname about my pants! Please?"

The boys laughed and pedaled off. Dale shouted, "Let's meet Saturday at eleven o'clock at the fort. I'll need to get out after eating for two days."

It was quite a sight to see the boys weaving back and forth as they rode down the street with rocks, turkeys, horns of plenty, and their instruments balanced in their hands. Dale thought, *What a great start to vacation. I wonder what Scout is doing?*

Chapter 10

# BASIC TRAINING

Artie was officially assigned to be Scout's handler, so he followed the dog through his official processing into the Army. Every soldier in the military has a record card, and dogs are no exception. Scout's card would keep track of his training and would later include his assignment in the Army.

The camp veterinarian, Dr. Franken, a kindly silver-haired man, came back to perform a more thorough examination. He took a blood sample from Scout and checked to make sure that he was in top condition. Scout had already had his rabies and distemper shots, so the vet didn't have to give him those injections.

The last step in the process was to tattoo a number in Scout's left ear and on his belly. Since dogs in the Dogs for Defense program would be working under rugged conditions, collars and dog tags were considered dangerous because they could get caught on fences and in underbrush. They also could fall off, which made tattooing the identification number a necessity so that an Army dog could always be identified, regardless of the situation.

Scout stood on the examination table while Dr. Franken lifted his ear. As the doctor reached for his instruments, Scout started to whine. Artie stepped over and gently stroked the dog's fur. "It's OK, boy, it'll just take a minute." Artie helped the doctor by holding Scout as the he tattooed the number C4602 on the dog's belly and inside his ear. After the last number was etched, Artie released his hold on the dog, which jumped up and shook himself. Scout was now an official member of the Army.

Scout had to wait two weeks in his quarantine kennel before he could begin basic training. While the dog waited, Artie attended classes run by experienced dog handlers who demonstrated techniques for teaching dog obedience. By the time Scout's quarantine and the classes were over, Artie was excited about trying out his newly acquired skills.

The next morning, Scout moved into his new kennel, a wooden structure covered with tarpaper approximately seven feet long by three feet wide. The kennels formed two long lines stretching the length of the barracks that housed the soldiers. Scout was assigned to number thirteen, his home for the next few months. At first, he sniffed the perimeter of the cage, and then looked at Artie, who smiled. Finally, Scout decided the kennel was all right and circled near the corner. The dog yawned and curled up, placing his head on his paws.

That afternoon Scout's official training began. Artie snapped on the dog's leash and led him to the grassy meadow opposite the barracks, where fifty other handlers with their dogs were jockeying for position. Artie was proud of the way Scout obeyed him as he selected a spot in the open-air classroom. The handlers kept the leashes short, as the dogs were anxious with this change of routine. One black-and-white Dalmatian kept barking despite repeated reprimands from his handler. Other dogs tugged on their leashes to sniff at the dog next to them. Once the dogs settled down a bit, the training began.

The commands were easy at first: *Sit, Stay, Come* when called. Next Scout learned to heel, which meant he had to walk or run with his right shoulder parallel to

Artie's left knee. Artie leaned over and stroked Scout's black-and-white fur. "You're the smartest dog at Fort Robinson," he said.

As the training progressed, Artie and Scout became more comfortable with one another. By the end of the second week of training, they were best friends.

Chapter 11

# SCOUT'S CHRISTMAS PRESENT

Saturday morning dawned with heavy, gray December clouds that had coated the town of Libertyville with several inches of fresh snow. Dale snuggled under the covers of his bed and thought of Scout. It had been four weeks since Dale had hugged his dog goodbye at the train depot. He especially noticed Scout's absence when he rode his bike home after school and was sad that his dog wasn't waiting at the front porch to greet him.

But the time passed quickly with Thanksgiving vacation, school, band, and nightly practice for the upcoming holiday concert. It was hard to believe that after weeks of waiting, the USO concert with Tommy Dorsey and the Andrews Sisters was just one day away. Dale had gotten a ticket for Sandra, so now the group numbered ten. The smell of freshly brewed coffee wafted up from the kitchen, reminding Dale that he was really hungry and breakfast was waiting.

As he slid into his seat, Dale noticed an envelope addressed to him propped up against a cup of steaming hot coffee.

"Go ahead, open it. It has your name on it," his grandmother said.

Dale noticed the postmark from Fort Robinson as he read aloud the outside of the envelope: "Master Dale Kingston." As he tore open the letter, he said, "I hope it's about Scout."

Dear Dale:

We are happy to advise you that your dog, with name, brand number, and breed as follows, has arrived at this Depot in good condition:

Scout Kingston

C4602

Border Collie

At this time, we are not able to predict your dog's adaptability to the rigors of Army training.

You will, of course, understand why the interests of military secrecy will be best served if further information is withheld from this point forward.

Thanking you for your generous donation at the time of this national emergency, I am,

Frank Sheffield, Commanding Officer
Fort Robinson, Nebraska

Dale sank back in the chair, relieved at last to have learned that Scout had arrived safely at Fort Robinson and was now in the process of basic training. As he laid the letter on the table, he noticed writing on the back of the typewritten letter. It read:

Dear Dale,

My name is Artie Klimza. I am assigned
to work with Scout as his handler.
I read the note that Scout brought
with him, and I promise you that
Scout will be properly taken care of.
He is a fine animal, and you should be
very proud of him.

Sincerely,
Artie Klimza
Private, U.S. Army

*Artie Klimza... I like that name,* thought Dale as he reread the small, neat handwriting. Dale felt comforted that Scout had a handler who would take the time to write him a note. As he finished reading, he heard his mom's jeep pull up outside. Excited by the fact that Scout was alive and well, he jumped up and raced to the back door just as his mom was entering.

"Slow down! What has you so excited?" his mom said as she closed the back door to keep out the cold.

"I heard from Artie about Scout."

"Who's Artie?" his mom said as she took the official letter and read it.

Dale took back the letter and turned it over. "Look, this is the Artie I was talking about. He's Scout's handler, and he wrote me a note."

Dale's mom read the handwritten note. "Well, I think that's wonderful news, and I agree that Artie sounds like a great handler."

"You know, Mom, Christmas is about two weeks away. Could we send Scout a Christmas present?"

"What did you have in mind?"

"Scout would probably like a big, juicy ham bone. I'll bet he doesn't get any bones at Fort Robinson."

Mother looked at Grandma, who was at the counter, suppressing a smile. Then she looked across the table at Dale's face and saw his earnest eyes. "Dale, I have a little money stashed away in the coffee can behind the flour tin. Why don't you go over to Shuller's Butcher Shop on Main Street and buy Scout the best, juiciest ham bone you can find. You tell Mr. Shuller who the bone is for, and I'm sure he'll help you get a good one. Make sure they wrap it in heavy wax paper; we want it to arrive in good shape. When you get home, we'll get a box and send it right away.

If we hurry, we can get it out before the mailman comes."
Dale jumped up and gave his mom a hug.

"By the way," Mom said, "this Artie sounds like a nice young man. Let's send him a piece of chocolate for being so nice to Scout." That's all Dale needed to hear as he forgot about breakfast, grabbed the money, put on his coat and boots, and trudged through the snow to Shuller's Butcher Shop.

When Dale returned, his cheeks were red from the strong north wind. Under his arm was a white package tied with string, and in his coat pocket was a chocolate bar for Artie. Grandpa had arrived home from work and was sitting in the kitchen when Dale entered and proudly laid the package on the table.

"Look what I got," Dale said as he untied the string and displayed his prize—a gleaming white bone with a large rounded end with hunks of ham still clinging to it. "Mr. Shuller helped me pick it out. He said that a great dog like Scout serving his country needed the best bone money could buy. What do you think?"

Grandma said, "Well, that's one of the best bones I've seen, and it'll make a great Christmas present. Let's get it all wrapped up and in the mail."

Dale rewrapped the bone, tied the string tightly

around it, and placed it carefully in the box his mother had found. He stuffed newspaper around the bone to keep it from bouncing and placed the candy bar on the top so it would be seen first. Dale ran up to his room to write a note to enclose in the package.

After sealing the box and setting it by the front door, Dale decided to practice his band music and wait for the mailman. He played long tones to warm up and then worked his way through each piece for the concert. When he had trouble remembering how the songs went, he counted rhythms out loud the way he had been taught by his grandfather. For the last ten minutes, he decided to work on the beginning of "Boogie Woogie Bugle Boy." During the last several weeks, Dale and his friends met at Bridget or Chrissy's house and listened to recordings. Dale knew the song by heart and had Mr. Jeffrey help him write out the notes to the opening bugle call. First, he counted the rhythm, and then he said the note names before he played the tune.

Just as he was beginning to sound like the recording, Dale was startled by a knock on the door. Putting his cornet down, Dale opened the door. Mr. Duckhorn, the mailman, was standing outside holding the package.

"Were you just playing 'Boogie Woogie Bugle Boy?' the mailman said. "You sure sound good."

"Thanks," Dale said. He pointed to the package. "I'm sending Scout a big bone for Christmas."

Mr. Duckhorn smiled and turned to continue his route. "I'll take good care of it for you."

Now that the bone was on its way, Dale had two things on his mind. First, he was starving, having skipped breakfast to get the bone; the other was the concert. Just then the phone rang.

"Dale, it's for you," Grandma said from the kitchen.

Dale took the phone and heard music playing in the background on the other end as Chrissy said hello.

"I could hear you practicing 'Boogie Woogie' and thought maybe you and the gang would like to come over this afternoon and listen to records before the concert tomorrow. We could also work out our swing dance moves so we're ready to dance at the concert. They always have dancing at the end."

"Great idea. I'll be over about three o'clock."

Dale hung up the phone and turned to his grandmother, who was setting his peanut butter sandwich and glass of milk on the table. "After I'm done with lunch, can we go in the living room and practice swing dancing?"

"I certainly could use the exercise."

Dale picked up the thick sandwich and took a huge bite.

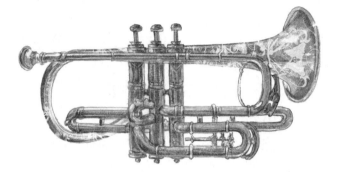

Chapter 12

# A NIGHT TO REMEMBER

The next evening, Dale buttoned his shirt, still warm from his mother's iron. He looked down to admire his freshly polished shoes. His grandfather said that at all military functions, the men make sure that their shoes are shined. On a night where there would be dancing, however, a little more elbow grease never hurt. Dale still had about thirty minutes until his friends gathered at his house before the concert and dance. He picked up a rag to add more polish to his shoes when the doorbell rang.

He heard his grandfather's say. "Come in, P. J. I knew you would be the first."

P. J. burst through the open door. "My mom drove me over early. She said she'd had enough of me talking about the big dance and asking her how much longer I had before I could go."

"As I always say, 'To be early is to be on time and to be on time is to be late.'"

P. J. pointed to his neck. "What do you think of my bow tie? I tied it myself."

Grandpa tilted his head and moved to straighten the tie a bit. "Not bad for your first time."

By this time, Dale had come up quietly behind his friend. He patted P. J.'s hair, which was slicked back for the occasion.

"Looks like you used a whole jar of Brylcreem."

P. J. turned red and took a handkerchief out of his pocket to wipe his brow.

Dale said, "That's OK. Sit down until everyone else gets here." Dale's mother came down the stairs dressed in her military uniform. Her face opened into a wide smile.

"Look at these young men. My, how they've grown up!"

P. J. jumped up, pushing out his chest. "Look, I even tied my own tie."

Before Dale's mother could comment, the doorbell rang again. Excited voices announced that the rest of the gang had arrived early as well.

As Dale opened the door, Bridget, Chrissy, and Sandra, dressed in brightly colored dresses with short wool coats, stood shivering on the porch. Tommy, Victor, Bobby, Karl, and Dave lined up behind them on the steps, casually leaning against the railings.

Dale was about to say how nice the girls looked, but Tommy pushed his way to the front, "Sorry we're early, but we couldn't wait."

Dale's grandfather and mother helped herd the group from the porch into the living room. "There must not be a white shirt left in Libertyville, let alone a bow tie," said Dale's mother.

Everyone laughed when they realized that all the boys had on the same black pants, white shirts, and red bow ties.

Just then Grandma entered the room and set a tray of freshly baked cookies and glasses of cold milk on the coffee table. "Thanks!" Victor said as he took a big bite of a chocolate chip cookie.

Chrissy added, "I spent the whole day getting ready with Bridget and Sandra, so I forgot to eat."

"Well, enjoy," Grandma said. "When I was young, I forgot to eat before my first dance, too."

The kids were enjoying the treat when they heard the sound of a loud truck coming down the street, followed by the grinding of brakes.

Tommy jumped up and looked out the picture window. "What's a big green army truck doing in front of your house, Dale?" Everyone crowded at the window to see the truck idling with its lights shining down the driveway of Dale's house.

Dale's mother stood, "Your ride to the dance has arrived."

"What do you mean?" Victor said.

"When General Packston heard all of you were coming, he thought that maybe a military truck would do for transportation to the concert."

Karl said, "What do you mean, 'will do'? To think we get to ride in a real army truck! Let's go!"

The gang put on coats and headed out to meet two uniformed soldiers. They snapped to attention and saluted as P. J. ran up to the truck.

"I'm First Lieutenant Dirk Swenson," the first soldier said. "I have orders from General Packston to escort you to and from the concert and dance." He extended his arm to Sandra, who stood next to P. J., and helped her up the ladder into the back of the tarp-covered truck. She found a seat on one of the wooden benches that lined the sides, followed by Chrissy and Bridget. "Gentlemen, you can climb in on your own."

The boys climbed the ladder and found seats next to the girls. "I'll leave the back flap open so you can see out.

Put your hands on the straps hanging from the sides and don't fall out," the lieutenant said.

"What do you mean, 'don't fall out'?" Sandra said, grasping Chrissy's hand.

"The ride will be bumpy, but you'll be fine. It will take about ten minutes." The soldier slammed the back gate and slid two large metal pins in slots in the side to lock it.

Karl said, "I can't believe we're in a real army truck!"

The girls sat quietly as the engine roared and the truck took off with a jerk. After a few minutes, Bridget said, "You know, this really is fun." Everyone began talking and laughing as the truck rumbled and bounced down the streets of Libertyville.

They all leaned as the truck rounded a curve and jerked to a stop. The truck had pulled into the Air Force base and stopped at the front gate. A soldier shined a flashlight into the back of the truck. His face was solemn as he examined the group. Finally, he stepped back and shouted to someone at the gate, "I count ten. That matches our orders from General Packston." He waved his flashlight to move the truck forward. "Let them in." The truck rumbled forward through the gate, passing lots of army vehicles and planes lining the runway.

"I never knew all this stuff was in here," Dave said.

Before anyone could respond, the truck lurched to a stop. Lieutenant Swenson appeared and unlocked the back gate. "It looks like no one fell out, so, mission accomplished. When the dance ends, report back to this truck." He extended his arm to Bridget. "Now enjoy the dance, and watch your step." Once everyone was safely out, the soldier turned and headed toward a large lighted building. "Follow me."

Victor ran behind the soldier so he could be first in line.

As they approached, the lieutenant opened a side door, bypassing the lines of people. "This way please."

Dale looked up at the high, arched ceiling. "This is the hangar where they store the planes," he said to Sandra.

The hangar was a massive building with a cement floor and a huge rounded roof supported by giant steel girders. Two bombers, a B-17 and a B-25, were parked along the back walls. Opposite the planes, two stages had been set up. The one on the left had hundreds of chairs lined in neat rows directly in front of it filled with excited people. The second stage had a large area roped off for dancing.

P. J. looked up, open-mouthed, at large cargo nets laden with balloons that hung above the dance floor. "I hope they drop them on us during the dance."

As the group threaded its way through the crowd, the lieutenant stopped and pointed to the ten chairs near the front. "These are your reserved seats. You'll be joined by General Packston and his wife in a few minutes." The soldier pointed to two seats on the end. "I'll return when the concert is over and escort you to the dance floor." The group selected their chairs, allowing Dale to have the chair next to General Packston. When they were seated, the soldier said, "Which one of you is Dale Kingston?

Dale raised his hand, "I am, sir."

"Please follow me." Lieutenant Swenson said.

Dave looked at Dale, who was sitting next to him. "What did you do?" But Dale had already jumped out of his chair to follow the lieutenant.

The girls leaned forward to ask what had happened when a tall, tanned man in a military uniform covered with medals stood in front of them.

"You must be Dale Kingston's friends. It's my pleasure to have you here this evening." He stepped aside. "May I introduce you to my wife and staff?"

The group stood up and shook the hands of each person introduced.

"I would like to commend you on how you look tonight. Please, let's sit down," the general said as the lights dimmed. He motioned for his wife to take a chair. "I think the concert is about to begin."

Bridget nudged Victor. "Where's Dale? The concert is starting."

Lights flooded the stage as the announcer welcomed everyone to the base and introduced General Packston, who stood and waved to the crowd.

Chrissy poked Bridget. "Where's Dale?" Bridget just shrugged her shoulders.

The announcer leaned into the microphone. "Let's welcome the Andrews Sisters, who will be accompanied by our own Jazz Orchestra under the direction of Sergeant Major Brad Hooper. Put your hands together for Laverne, Maxene, and Patty: the Andrews Sisters!" The three sisters pranced onstage dressed in Army nurse corps uniforms. Chrissy grabbed P. J.'s hand and squeezed. "I love their sequined platform shoes!"

The crowd erupted into applause as the band opened with "Don't Sit under the Apple Tree." As the song ended, the audience roared its approval, and Laverne held up her hand as she stepped to the mike.

"On behalf of Maxene and Patty, I thank you for that warm reception. And how about our backup band tonight? Aren't they the cat's meow?" The audience cheered.

Maxene sidled up to her sister at the mike. "As all of you probably know, we wrote a little song called 'Boogie Woogie Bugle Boy.'"

Chrissy elbowed P. J., "Where's Dale? I don't want him to miss this number!"

Laverne took back the mike. "Does anyone remember the first two verses of the song?" Victor jumped up and yelled, "Yes!" The sisters smiled down from the stage as Victor looked around and realized he was the only one standing. Laverne winked at her young fan as the crowd laughed.

"We found out there'd been a huge fire at the Conn Instrument plant. At first we thought we'd have to cancel our concert." Then Patty grabbed the mike, "But General Packston told us about a young man who saved the factory and the air base by playing his bugle." Maxene leaned in and said, "So we're not only going to dedicate this song to him, but"—she turned to the side of the stage and motioned—"we're going to bring him onstage right now and have him join us on this number." The gang looked over just as Dale hesitantly walked onstage and toward the Andrews Sisters, his gold-plated cornet glinting in the bright lights.

Chrissy, Bridget, and Sandra jumped to their feet

as Maxene said, "Let's hear it for Libertyville's own swinging bugle boy, Dale Kingston." Dale blushed as the three sisters gave him a group hug.

Maxene came back to the mike and held up her hand to quiet the crowd. "Dale, are you ready to swing with us?" She held the mike for him to answer.

"Yes, ma'am!" Dale pointed to the front row. "I'd like to dedicate this to my best friend, P.J., who helped me save the factory." Dale confidently put his horn to his lips.

"All right, let's do it." Maxene turned to Dale and started to snap her fingers to set the tempo. "Ah-one, ah-two, ah-one, two, three."

The opening bugle call of the song came out of Dale's cornet in a clear tone, just as he had practiced.

Chrissy screamed to Bridget over the crowd, "He sounds just like the recording!" The crowd roared, and the sisters leaned in, singing in perfect three-part harmony.

*He was a famous trumpet man from out Chicago way;*
*He had a boogie style that no one else could play.*
*He was the top man at his craft,*
*But then his number came up, and he was gone with*
*     the draft.*
*He's in the army now, blowing reveille;*
*He's the boogie woogie bugle boy of Company B.*

On the second verse Bridget, Chrissy, and Sandra mouthed the words.

*They made him blow a bugle for his Uncle Sam;*
*It really brought him down because he could not*
*     jam.*
*The captain seemed to understand,*
*Because the next day the cap' went out and drafted*
*     a band.*
*And now the company jumps when he plays*
*     reveille;*
*He's the boogie woogie bugle boy of Company B.*

When the final song of the concert ended, the announcer said, "Let's keep this party going and start the dancing! Mr. Dorsey, are you ready?" The Tommy Dorsey Orchestra began playing as the crowd surged onto the dance floor.

Lieutenant Swenson made his way to the reserved section with Dale following closely behind. The girls hugged Dale and the boys slapped him on the back.

"Why didn't you tell us?" P. J. said over the music.

"I was afraid I'd get too nervous."

Chrissy put her arm around Dale's shoulder. "I could hear you practicing that song all the time, and now I know why."

"Enough about me. Let's see if we can remember our swing-dance moves." He grabbed Chrissy's hand and they disappeared onto the dance floor.

Following Dale's lead, Tommy pulled Sandra's arm and Victor escorted Bridget onto the dance floor. With all of the girls taken, P. J. looked at Dave and said, "There's no way I'm dancing with you!" Just then, Dave's eyes widened, and P. J. felt a tap on his shoulder. He spun around to find Maxene, who leaned over to P. J.'s ear and whispered, "I heard how you got your nickname and think you must be a fun person. Would you dance with me?"

P. J. stood transfixed with his mouth open. Dale spun Chrissy around and poked his friend on the shoulder.

P. J. tucked in his shirt, puffed out his chest, and bowed. "It's my pleasure," he said, and he and Maxene began jitterbugging to the sounds of Dorsey's orchestra as hundreds of balloons fell from the ceiling.

When the music ended, Lieutenant Swenson found the group. "It's time to get you home, so please follow me." The group wound its way through the crowd of military personnel. The girls climbed into the back of the truck followed by the boys. The lieutenant slammed the gate closed, the engine roared to life, and the truck lurched forward.

The group laughed and talked as the truck stopped every few minutes to let each one off at his or her home. Finally, just P. J., Dale, and Chrissy were the last ones on the truck. The truck roared to a stop in front of P. J.'s home.

P. J. stood and thanked Dale for mentioning him onstage. He re-tucked his shirt and gave the soldier a salute before climbing down from the truck and running up to his house.

The truck rumbled forward, the engine straining as it slowly made its way up Simpson Hill.

Dale and Chrissy sat quietly, thoughts of the evening swirling in their heads. Just then the truck hit a large bump, and Chrissy flew across into Dale's arms. She looked up shyly into Dale's eyes.

"Don't worry, I wouldn't let anything happen to you," Dale said as he realized he didn't want to let go of her.

Chrissy said, "I had so much fun dancing with you. I wish tonight would never end."

They were still looking at each other when they heard First Lieutenant Dirk Swenson clear his throat. They straightened, and Chrissy smoothed her dress to stand up. "Last stop, all out," he said as he looked aside and unlocked the back gate.

The two let go of each other's hands and climbed out of the truck. The soldier shook Dale's hand. "It was my pleasure to have served you tonight," he said before he turned and jumped back in the truck.

Dale walked Chrissy across the street. Just as Chrissy put her foot on the first step of the porch, the light snapped on. Chrissy waved good-bye and ran up the steps.

Dale slowly walked back to his house where his grandfather was waiting on the porch.

"From the looks of things, I'll bet you had one special evening," Grandpa said, standing. "Come in and tell me all about it." He put his arm around Dale's shoulder.

Chapter 13

# THE GREAT ESCAPE

Fort Robinson was usually a windy, snowy place the week before Christmas. This year, however, the chill had lifted, and the temperature was in the fifties. Scout had adjusted to his military routine with ease, and Artie was pleased with the dog's training. As he sat on the steps of the barracks with Scout at his side, he examined a large, brown package addressed in neat block letters. He cut the string with his army knife and gently unwrapped the package. Inside was a handwritten note, a smaller package wrapped in white butcher paper with Scout's name on it, and a large piece of chocolate.

"I think you have a letter from your master," he said to the dog. Scout's head popped up, and he barked twice as Artie began to read aloud.

Dear Artie,

Thanks for writing to me about Scout. I'm glad that he arrived safely and that you're taking good care of him. He's a great dog, and I hope he does what you ask.

Scout likes bones, so I've sent him a big ham bone as a Christmas present. I hope that's OK with the Army. My mom thought you would like the chocolate bar.

Thanks for taking good care of my dog.

Sincerely,
Dale Kingston

P.S. When you give Scout the bone, can you give him a big hug and tell him it's from me?

Artie folded the note and inserted it back into the envelope. He decided that after Christmas he would write to Dale to tell him how Scout was progressing in his training. Scout sat up, his tail wagging, as Artie unwrapped the paper around the large bone. "Here boy, this is from Dale. Merry Christmas!"

At the mention of Dale's name, Scout turned his head and barked twice before lying down to gnaw eagerly on the end of the bone.

Artie leaned back on the steps, enjoying the rare, warm December sun. It reminded him of being home on his Montana cattle ranch with his dog, Rusty, enjoying the sun and his pet's company.

Scout was halfway through the bone when Sergeant Stafford approached.

"Artie, I've been thinking," he said as he pointed to the far northwest corner of the camp. "That fence is rather weak, and some sections need to be replaced. We're a bit short-handed. I want you to take care of the job for me."

"Yes, sir. I'll get right on it this morning." Sergeant Stafford nodded his approval and made his way back to the officer's headquarters.

Artie put the note and the chocolate in his knapsack for later and picked up the ham bone before he led Scout back to the kennel. He opened the fenced door and Scout ran in. Artie set down the gift from Dale. "Scout, take your time with that bone. When I'm done fixing the fence, we'll go for a run." Scout barked twice and circled down to continue working on the bone.

Artie went back to the barracks to get his tools where he ran into Joe, his bunkmate. "Could you do me a favor? I haven't had a chance to exercise Scout yet. If I'm not done fixing this broken fence in two hours, would you take him out and run him?"

Joe was a very agreeable guy. "Be glad to, Artie," he said as he tucked his blanket under his mattress. Joe and Artie had been bunkmates since they had arrived at Fort Robinson. Joe had the top bunk and Artie had the bottom. The two men seemed to be total opposites. Joe was short and round with a dark complexion, while Artie was tall, lanky, and fair-skinned, but they had two things in common, and that was a love of dogs and the Army regulation crew cut.

"Thanks," Artie said as he collected his tools and set off for the far northwest section of camp. While he walked over the worn grass of the training field, Artie thought about how lucky he was to be in the Army doing a job he loved: working with dogs. He arrived at the fence, set down his toolbox and shovel, and inspected the posts. Just as Sergeant Stafford had said, two wooden posts had nearly rotted away and needed to be replaced. "It's a good thing there are no classes today," Artie muttered as he took wire cutters out of the toolbox. "I'll have to remove this section of fence to put in the new posts."

Artie clipped away at one side of the fence, then the other side, leaving an eight-foot section open. Next he picked up his shovel and dug into the soft, muddy ground.

"We're lucky to have this warm weather," he thought, "otherwise we'd have to wait until spring. These posts wouldn't last through the first big snow."

The soldier finished digging a hole around the first post. He wiggled the rotten wood back and forth until he loosened it, and then hefted the post out. Laying it aside, he moved to the next post and did the same.

"I'll use the old post to measure the new ones." As he lifted the post to his shoulder, he glanced at his watch. "Wow, that took over an hour and a half! I'd better hurry if I want to get this done and back to exercise Scout." Artie hurried to the lumberyard to get the replacement posts he needed, thinking it would only be a few minutes before he could close the eight-foot hole in the fence. Since no dogs were out, he reasoned that it would be OK to leave the open hole for the short time it would take to fix the posts.

Meanwhile, Joe had gone over to Scout's kennel. The dog had finished his Christmas present and was napping in a patch of warm sunlight.

"Hey, boy! Let's go for a run." He stood up to open the door to the cage. Scout looked quizzically at the man, for usually Artie was the only one who opened the door. Joe hooked on a leash and patted the dog on the neck. "Let's go for a run."

By the second lap around the camp, Joe was sweating, breathing heavily, and ready for a rest. Scout strained at his leash as if to indicate that he could go for one more lap.

This time, Joe led Scout behind the mess hall so they wouldn't have to run all the way around the camp. As they rounded the corner, they found themselves in a soapy quagmire. Kitchen workers had just thrown out several buckets of soapy water used to clean the mess hall floor, creating a sloppy pool of mud. Before Joe could stop, his feet came out from under him, and he landed on his back in the mud. Scout decided that the mud looked like fun, and began rolling around on his back. Joe sat upright and found himself looking directly into two big, brown eyes set in a mass of mud-covered, matted fur.

"Just look at us, Scout. We can't let Artie see us like this!" Grabbing Scout's leash, the private headed for the kennel so that they could both rinse off. Joe found a hose coiled next to the building. "Sit, Scout," Joe said as he unhooked the dog's leash. Scout warily sat down and whimpered while the soldier turned on the hose. Water shot from the hose with such force that the metal nozzle flew out of Joe's hand. Scout jumped back as the menacing nozzle waved back and forth on the ground like a cobra ready to strike. Before Joe could regain control of the hose, the nozzle smacked Scout on the nose. With a yelp, the dog took off around the barracks and out of sight. Joe ran helplessly after the animal, waving his arms and pleading for the dog to stop. He yelled to some privates standing by the mess hall to join in the pursuit, but Scout was too fast for them. As the dog raced toward the far corner of the camp, he spied a large opening in the fence and made a beeline for it.

Artie heard the commotion as he left the lumberyard with the new fence posts atop his shoulders. By the time he reached the fence, he found Joe and some other soldiers pointing off in the distance. On the horizon was a distant black-and-white speck.

"What's going on?" Artie said. Joe, still out of breath, said, "Scout's AWOL!"

Chapter 14

# A DESPERATE SEARCH

Artie dropped the posts and yelled to the other soldiers to take over the job of repairing the fence. He and Joe sprinted toward the motor pool where all the camp vehicles were parked. Knowing they needed a requisition to use a jeep, they found a sergeant on duty and told their story.

"OK, you can have one, but you'd better take a jeep. You may have to go off-road, and nothing stops a jeep."

"Thanks," Artie said as he jumped behind the wheel of one of the mud-covered, topless vehicles as Joe scrambled into the passenger seat. The engine roared to life and they wheeled out of the compound, pausing briefly at the guard gate before speeding down the road to search the fields for signs of Scout.

"Take a right here," Joe said over the sound of the wind and the drone of the engine. Artie turned sharply, throwing gravel and dirt everywhere as they continued down the rutted roads outside the camp. Joe held on tightly to the front windshield frame so he would not fall out as the jeep bounced down the road. When they reached the northwest corner of the camp, Artie slammed on the brakes. As the dust settled, he could see the fence opening where Scout had made his escape from camp.

Scratching his forehead, Artie turned to Joe, "We have to think like a dog. Where would a scared dog run?"

Joe looked perplexed. He, too, realized that Scout could be just about anywhere on the Nebraska plains.

Artie revved the jeep and the two men took off, driving up and down the country roads, searching for any signs of movement. Suddenly some cornstalks in a roadside field swayed, and the pair got their hopes up until they realized the movement was from a coyote in search of food. Disappointed, Artie and Joe continued on their quest. For the next hour they combed nearly twenty square miles. They had almost given up hope when, in the distance, Joe spotted a dog. "There he is!" he said, pointing to an animal running along the edge of a field.

Without hesitation Artie gunned the jeep off the road, down a shallow ditch, and up into the cornstalks. Mud and cornstalks flew everywhere, but Artie and Joe kept their eyes focused on the animal. "It sure looks like him," Artie said as the jeep bounced over ruts in the field. Joe agreed as they closed in on the fleeing dog.

The animal stopped for a moment, then took off when he realized the vehicle was coming toward him.

"He's veering left, toward that creek ahead," Joe said.

"This machine will handle anything," Artie said as he slammed the vehicle into a lower gear and ground down a hill to the muddy creek below. The jeep slowed for a second as it hit the mud and eased into the creek. Then Artie hit the accelerator, throwing mud and water everywhere. Finally the tires caught hold and began to chew into the earth and up the other side of the embankment.

"I told you we'd get him," Artie said as they gained on the running dog.

The dog took a sharp right and headed for a farmyard up the field from the creek. Artie revved the engine and followed. The dog ran past the farmhouse, ducked behind the corner, and disappeared. The jeep skidded in the gravel beside the house just as the dog ran into the barn through the open door. The men, covered in mud, jumped out of the vehicle and ran toward the barn. They stopped short when a man stepped out of the shadowy interior. "Hey, what are you two doing?"

"My dog just ran into your barn."

"Your dog? The only dog that ran in here is one of mine. Name is Shep."

Artie didn't want to be pushy, but he was certain that the farmer was mistaken and that Scout was hiding in the barn.

"Can we just take a look? We're from Fort Robinson, and one of our dogs escaped."

"I'm sorry, men. With all the mud, I wasn't sure who you were. My name is Lars Overhoffen. Go ahead and make sure that's not your dog."

Artie and Joe entered the barn and saw that it was lined with stalls. A horse whinnied as the two men walked, peering into each stall. Finally, they found the dog lying underneath some straw in the last stall.

"Scout," Artie said. He was filled with joy and relief that he had finally found his missing friend. When the dog lifted his head, however, Artie felt sick to his stomach as he realized that there was a chance that the dog was not Scout. He had the same black-and-white markings but he was covered with mud, so Artie could not be sure of the dog's identity. But he clung to the possibility that this animal was Scout.

The farmer stepped beside Artie and Joe. Artie turned and shook his head. "It looks like him, but with all the mud, it's hard to know for sure. I have one way to tell. Each dog has a tattooed number in its left ear and also on its stomach. If I can look at his ear or stomach, I'll know for sure."

Lars rubbed his chin. "I wouldn't touch his ears, but I'll see if he'll let me scratch his stomach. That way you'll be able to see if he has the tattoo number."

"Thanks. I just want to make sure."

"Come here, Shep. Come on, good dog." The dog slowly crawled out from under the straw and cautiously approached the three men.

Lars knelt next to the animal, and the dog instinctively rolled over, knowing he would get a belly rub.

As the farmer scratched, Artie searched desperately for a tattoo, but the dog's pink belly was barren. "Sorry for your trouble, Mr. Overhoffen."

"I'll keep my eye out for your dog. What'd you say his name was?"

Artie and Joe turned to return to the jeep. "His name is Scout, and he's a black-and-white Border Collie."

As he started the engine, Artie's thoughts flashed to a young boy in Libertyville, Indiana who had written him a letter asking him to take special care of his dog. He knew he had failed miserably in keeping that promise.

The next week Artie spent every bit of his free time scouring the fields and towns surrounding Fort Robinson for signs of the dog. He hung up signs in town offering a small reward for any information on Scout's whereabouts. As the days passed and the weather turned cold again, Artie knew the odds of finding the dog were diminishing. He vowed that he would keep his promise to Dale and never give up his search for the missing dog. Now he had to write the boy a letter and explain what had happened.

Chapter 15

# FINAL PREPARATIONS

It had been a week and a half since Dale's performance with the Andrews Sisters. Everyone was still talking about the dance, but now the excitement was building toward their first concert, just four days before Christmas. The band had worked for the past two weeks on cleaning up notes, playing with dynamics, and learning how to perform in public.

On several occasions, the gang had gathered at either Dale's or Bridget's house to practice. Mr. Jeffrey stressed that the fun of music was practicing together. Each time they did, they took turns conducting. They learned to fix each other's mistakes without getting mad. They decided that if someone made a mistake, then the group would discuss the problem and solve it. Mr. Jeffrey had reminded them that fixing mistakes is part of learning the music and not a personal criticism. Finally, the day of the last rehearsal had arrived. Everyone was very focused and excited that they would finally be able to perform in the concert that night.

Mr. Jeffrey asked his students to invite their friends and family to the concert so that they would have a large audience. He also encouraged them to make concert posters and distribute them throughout the town.

On the way to school the chilly, gray morning of the concert, Dale and P. J. decided to ride through downtown Libertyville to see the posters. "Which one is yours?" Dale said as he searched the store windows.

"You mean you can't tell?"

P. J. pointed to Walker's Hardware Store. In the center of the window was a large, colorful poster featuring Santa playing a tuba with details about the concert pouring out of the bell like notes.

Dale pulled up to the window. "What a great idea! I should have guessed that one was yours."

"I thought that if Santa played an instrument, it would be a tuba."

Dale laughed, and the two continued to school. Once they arrived, they helped set up the chairs and stands and then warmed up.

The room quieted when Mr. Jeffrey stepped on the podium. "It's very important that we practice like we are performing for an audience. We can't expect a great performance if we don't practice well. Each rehearsal is a concert." Every eye was on Mr. Jeffrey as he continued his instructions. "I'd like you to put your music in concert order on the right side of your folder as I announce each number. Then I'd like to run each piece straight through with no stopping, no matter what happens. At the end of each piece, we'll talk about what to fix before moving on to the next one."

Tommy said, "Do you mean that no matter what happens, we won't stop?"

"Musicians don't stop in concerts for mistakes. Whatever happens, we'll adjust as we go because that's the fun of a live performance. You have one chance at a concert, so make that one time memorable for your audience, yourself, and your fellow musicians. A concert is the ultimate team effort."

Dale looked across the band at Chrissy and Bridget. He could see as they leaned forward in their chairs, their eyes focused on Mr. Jeffrey, that they were determined to make this first concert great.

Mr. Jeffrey called out the pieces, and the band members put their music in the correct order. Then the band played each piece. "Don't put your instrument down until I put my hand down. We want the audience to enjoy the last note of the piece. Any movement from you takes away from that moment."

The band continued to play each song and then Mr. Jeffrey asked them what they wanted to fix. "I think the cornets are playing too loud and covering up my horn part," Victor said to Dale and Sandra.

"I want everyone to watch my left hand for the dynamics. Victor's right; you're concentrating so hard on the notes, you're not playing the music." Mr. Jeffrey demonstrated how his left hand pushed down when he wanted the band to play softer. "Let's play a concert B-flat and hold it out. Then I want you to play the dynamics I indicate with my left hand."

The band played the note, then Mr. Jeffrey motioned upward with his left palm for more volume. Then he turned his hand over so that his palm faced everyone, indicating less volume as his hand moved downward... then louder... then softer... then louder... then softer. Soon Mr. Jeffery was going from loud to soft so fast that his hand just waved back and forth. He stopped the band, and everyone started laughing.

"I hope that this exercise shows how important it is to focus on the conductor's hand and play the dynamics. Do you think we can play the next song with dynamics?"

The band played, paying particular attention to the dynamics. Mr. Jeffrey was pleased as he set his baton on the stand.

"Dynamics give the music emotion and feeling."

Bridget turned around and caught Dale's eye. She looked at him for a moment before turning back.

"Now I want to practice coming onstage in your rows. An orderly entrance sets the tone for how a group plays." Everyone gathered their instruments and music and went backstage to practice filing in. They waited until Bobby, the first-chair clarinetist, sat down before the rest of the band sat down. After several practices, Bobby started to sit down, but when he was almost down—and everyone else was almost down as well—he popped back up. The band stood back up quickly. Everyone laughed. "Bobby, this isn't a game."

"Sorry, Mr. Jeffrey. I just wanted to see if they were paying attention, like what you did with the dynamics. I promise I won't do it at the concert."

At the end of the rehearsal, Mr. Jeffrey reminded the boys to wear dark pants, a white shirt and tie, and black shoes. The girls were told to wear a dark skirt, white blouse, and dark shoes with bobby socks. The band was expected to meet in the gym at six-fifteen sharp.

The rest of the school day flew by. As everyone packed up at the end of the day, Bridget slipped over to Dale when no one was looking.

"I've got a present for you," she said, and put a package wrapped in red-and-green paper in his knapsack. "Wait until you get home to open it."

Dale watched as Bridget joined Chrissy and Sandra for the walk home. Then he felt an elbow jab him in the back. "Come on, Dale," P. J. said. "Let's ride downtown and look at the concert posters again. I forgot to see which one was yours." The boys ran down the steps of Emerson School and across the windy playground to the bike rack.

"Let's race," Dale said.

The boys pedaled furiously to Main Street, and Dale skidded to a stop in front of Bailey's Barber Shop.

P. J., breathing hard and sweating despite the frosty weather, slid to a stop next to his friend. Once he caught his breath, P. J. said, "I should've guessed that one was yours."

"Why would you have guessed that?"

P. J. pointed to the picture of a boy on a toboggan playing a cornet. A black-and-white dog was pulling the toboggan. In bold letters, the poster read, "Slide Over to the Emerson School Concert."

"Come on, P. J. I need to eat and get ready for our first concert."

P. J. nodded and turned toward his home.

Dale rode up Simpson Hill thinking about the concert poster and how much he missed Scout. As he rounded the corner at the top of the hill, he remembered the present Bridget had given him at the end of the day. He parked his bike and ran into the house.

Chapter 15

# THE MOST DIFFICULT LETTER

Artie sat cross-legged on his bunk in the barracks. It had been days since Scout's escape, and Artie couldn't stop blaming himself.

"How could I have been so careless? Why hadn't I waited to cut the fence until after I'd made the new posts?"

The questions kept circling in his mind as he thought of several ways he could have prevented the escape. But no matter how much Artie wished the events of the past could be erased, the fact remained that Scout was gone.

The door to the barracks pushed open and Joe stepped in. He still felt embarrassed that he had caused the loss of his friend's dog. Trying to be lighthearted, Joe rubbed his hands together.

"Brrrr! It's getting cold out there." Even Joe's jovial manner couldn't lift Artie's heavy spirits.

"Hey, come on... I know you're upset by Scout's escape, but I'm as much to blame as you are. I feel terrible, too, and now we're both going to feel even worse."

"What could make me feel worse?" Artie said, and then he saw the knapsack that Dale had sent with Scout. "Why'd you have to bring that in here?"

"The Colonel ordered me to clean out Scout's kennel since more dogs are coming in. I packed up his things, put them in the knapsack and thought you'd want them instead of me throwing them away."

"I'm sorry for being so grumpy. I'm glad you didn't throw them away."

Joe laid the knapsack on the bunk next to Artie and went to put some more wood in the big, black, wrought iron stove.

Artie opened the knapsack and was reminded of how fond he had become of Scout. He took out the ball and remembered how he and Scout played during their free time. Next he took out Scout's leash, military message collar, and pillow, and then he found at the bottom of the pack the one thing that he didn't want to find. It was the handwritten note that Dale had sent with Scout.

Artie opened the envelope, took out the note, and re-read the letter. He held the note in his hands for several minutes before turning to Joe. "How am I ever going to tell this young man that put his trust in me that his dog is missing and it's my fault?"

Joe finished putting wood on the fire and sat down on the bunk next to Artie. "Maybe you don't have to tell him. Just have the commander write a letter; he'll explain the whole mix-up. Then you're off the hook."

"You don't understand, Joe. I let this boy down. I promised to take care of his dog. I have to be the one to tell him Scout is missing."

"Suit yourself," Joe said, as he stood up and stepped toward the door. "But you're only making it harder on yourself."

The door slammed shut, and Artie was alone in the barracks. Cold metal bunks lined each wall, each bed indistinguishable from the next with its regulation pea-green army blanket tucked in precisely at each corner. The light from the afternoon winter sun played on the bare wood floor. Artie shivered as he felt the cold creeping in under the door. As he sat on his bed, he had never felt so alone and homesick.

He kept his paper and pens in the trunk at the foot of his bed. Lifting the lid, Artie sorted through his belongings, took out some paper and sat back on the bed to write the most difficult letter he had ever written. Images of Artie as a boy of eleven romping through the barn with his dog Rusty flashed through his mind as he wrote, "Dear Dale," at the top of the page.

Before he continued, he tried to put himself in the eleven-year-old's shoes. *"How would I feel if I had gotten a letter that Rusty was missing? That some stupid Army guy had let him escape?"* Gritting his teeth, Artie set to writing the tale of Scout's escape.

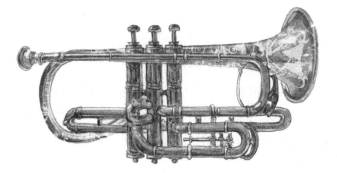

Chapter 17

## FIRST CONCERT

Dale walked into the kitchen to find his mother, grandmother, and grandfather at the table. Setting his knapsack in the corner, he asked why they were home so early.

"We got off work early, so we could eat together before your concert," said Mom. Grandpa chimed in, "I think the whole town is coming tonight." Grandma nodded. "Now go wash up. We're having a light dinner so you're not too full to play. After the concert, we'll have your favorite dessert, pumpkin pie."

Dale took the stairs two at a time to wash his hands. When he returned, a big bowl of chicken soup with homemade noodles was steaming at his place next to a cold roast beef sandwich.

"I wish we had more concerts if I get my favorite foods," Dale said as he plunged his spoon into the soup.

During dinner the family discussed how the last rehearsal before the concert went, what songs they were playing, and how nice all the posters looked in the various storefronts.

"I liked them all," Grandpa said, "but the one I liked the best was the one with Santa holding a tuba saying, Merry Tuba, Merry Tuba and a Merry Tuba to All. Was that P. J.'s idea?"

"I think it's the best one, too. How'd you like mine?"

"Your drawing of Scout looked just like him. I'll bet he really appreciated that bone you sent him."

"May I be excused to get ready for the concert?"

"Yes you may," his mother said, "I want to leave here at five-forty-five sharp so you're on time for the warm-up."

Before Grandpa could say anything, they all said together, "To be early is to be on time and to be on time is to be late."

"Well, well... it looks like I've trained you well," Grandpa said. "Now go get ready."

Dale grabbed his knapsack, ran up the stairs, and closed his door. He sat on his bed, opened the knapsack, and took out the neatly wrapped present from Bridget. He opened the note that was attached to the present.

Dear Dale,

I wanted to thank you for making it possible for us all to start band. I thought a long time about what to get you for Christmas. I hope you like it. I made it myself.

♥ Bridget

Dale tore open the paper, and in the wrapping was a beautiful red tie with an embroidered gold cornet on the front. He examined the detail of the white pearl valve caps, the perfectly shaped mouthpiece and the intricate tubing. Touching the embroidery, he felt the fine stitching that almost looked like a painting. "I'll bet there isn't another tie in the world like this one," he thought as he jumped up to show his family.

"Who did that beautiful embroidery?" Grandmother said, closely examining the stitching.

"You know Bridget, don't you? Can I wear it to the concert tonight? Mr. Jeffrey said we had to wear a tie."

Grandfather said, "Of course you may. One of the signs that you're turning into a young man is being able to tie your own tie. I'll teach you before we go. Now finish dressing."

Dale went back to his room and put on his white shirt, black pants, and freshly shined black shoes. When he returned to the living room, his grandfather had one of his old ties in his hand.

"I thought I was going to wear my new tie."

"You are. We're going to practice on this old one so we don't wrinkle the new one. Once you can tie the old one, you can tie the new one before we go."

For the next twenty minutes the two practiced tying Grandpa's old tie. First Grandpa demonstrated, and then he had Dale tie it himself. At first, Dale couldn't get the hang of it, but then Grandpa reminded him about the Boy Scout knots he had learned to tie.

Once he realized he was familiar with the type of knot, he had the old tie tied in no time. Dale glanced at the clock. "Can I tie Bridget's tie now?"

Grandpa agreed, and Dale tied the new tie. Grandpa made a slight adjustment. "Look in the mirror and see what you think."

Dale stood on his tiptoes in front of the mirror in the hallway and admired the new tie. Grandpa pointed to his watch, Dale grabbed his cornet, and everyone piled into the car for the short ride to the school. As they pulled into the parking lot, dozens of cars were arriving. Dale leaned on the front seat. "Look at all the people! You'd better hurry in and get a seat in the auditorium while I go to the gym and get ready."

"Good luck," his mother said as he jumped out of the car.

When Dale got to the gym, other band members were arriving and sitting down to warm up. He took his jacket off and turned around to take his seat. Victor said, "Where'd you get that tie?"

Before he could answer, Dale noticed that Bridget put her finger to her lips, making a "shh" signal.

"I got it from someone very special."

Bridget smiled and resumed warming up her saxophone.

As the other students arrived, Dale's tie became the topic of conversation, but he never told that Bridget had made it for him.

When Mr. Jeffrey stepped onto the podium everyone stopped playing and listened to his final concert instructions. "It's time to think only of our performance

and the job each of you must do to make this a great
night."

Mr. Jeffrey tuned each instrument, and then had the
band play a group warm-up. At precisely six-fifty the
director asked the first clarinetist to lead the way into the
auditorium.

Bobby chuckled when Mr. Jeffrey asked him to have
the band sit just once. "Don't worry, Mr. Jeffrey. I'll do it
right." At the door to the auditorium, Bobby stopped and
waited for the signal for the band to enter.

When Mr. Jeffrey's watch read six fifty-five, he said,
"Take them in, Bobby. They're all yours."

Bobby straightened up, opened the door, and led the
band onto the brightly lit stage. The audience applauded
as the band members took their seats. Squinting into the
audience, Dale could see that all of the seats were filled
and people were standing in the back and on the sides of
the auditorium. In the front row sat Mr. Greenleaf, the
owner of the Conn factory, Joe Maddy, the president of
Interlochen Music Camp, and General Packston and his
wife. P. J. bowed his tuba at the volunteer firemen who
were seated behind a row of soldiers from the base.

Everyone adjusted their stands and did not wave to
the audience. All eyes were on Bobby while they waited

for him to sit down. Bobby looked back at the band and sat down. The band followed, making last minute adjustments to their stands and chairs while they got the first selection out.

Principal Prenty strode to the microphone. "Welcome to Emerson School's first band concert." With a nod to the first row, his voice low and strong, he thanked Mr. Greenleaf for making the band program a reality through his donation of instruments. Mr. Greenleaf stood to a thunderous applause and waved to the audience.

"I'd also like to recognize the two students responsible for saving the factory, Dale Kingston and Charlie Walsh. Dale stood up, but P. J. just sat there until Tommy poked him. "Don't you remember your name?"

P. J. popped up and said while he waved, "I don't think anyone has called me Charlie for months."

"Without any further delay, let's bring out our director of bands, Mr. Jeffrey."

As the conductor came onstage, the band stamped their feet, a sign of respect that Mr. Jeffrey taught them.

He bowed to the audience and then stepped onto the podium, smiling proudly at his students who had worked so hard to prepare this concert. After the first song, "American Eagle," the crowd erupted in applause, and

Mr. Jeffrey pointed at Bobby to stand, followed by the rest of the band. Sandra nudged Dale. "He must really think we did a good job if he's having us stand." Dale nodded, and when the applause subsided, Mr. Jeffrey pointed at Bobby to sit down and get ready for the next number.

Just before the final number, Mr. Jeffrey spoke to the audience. "I'd like to thank everyone for coming to our concert and supporting these fine young musicians. The students have worked very hard, and you can tell that their effort has paid off. Please join us in the lobby for punch and cookies after the concert." Then he returned to the podium for the final piece.

On the last note, Mr. Jeffrey held his hand out longer than normal. To the students' surprise, he began the dynamic exercise by holding his left hand low so that the note began softly. Gradually, as his left hand moved higher and higher, the band played louder. When his hand was at the highest point and the band was at its loudest point, he held the note before cutting the band off. The note rang through the auditorium, the band not moving so they could enjoy the lush sound. When Mr. Jeffrey lowered his arms, the crowd broke into applause. He bowed and had Bobby and the band stand. "Thanks for playing your hearts out," he said.

Dale took his time in the gym before going to the reception. He made sure to empty the spit and oil his valves before setting his cornet in the velvet-lined case. He thought he was alone in the gym when a soft hand tapped him on the shoulder. He turned to see Bridget behind him.

"Thanks for not telling that I made that tie for you," she said, "It means a lot to me that you wore it for our first concert."

"The fact that you took the time to make it for me is really special."

He looked into her clear blue eyes, and was about to say something when P. J. burst through the door, "Come on, you're missing the food!"

Dale took Bridget's hand. "Let's go. We can't keep the gang waiting."

Chapter 18

# BAD NEWS

The vacation days between Christmas and New Years were some of the best that Dale could remember. The gang spent every day sledding down Simpson Hill on the new toboggan that Dale got for Christmas.

Dale had asked for the toboggan many times during the past year, hoping he could convince his mother and grandparents to buy it for him. On every occasion he could, he would bring up the present and remind them of what he wanted. His last hint had been the day before Christmas Eve. That night a big storm blanketed the city of Libertyville with eight inches of snow, the perfect gift for every child.

Dale remembered looking out of the living room picture window on Christmas Eve morning, "I'll bet a toboggan would go really fast in all this snow."

Mother winked at Grandfather. "Well, you don't have one, so don't get your hopes up. Money is tight with the war and all."

"She's right, Dale," Grandpa said.

"I understand. Whatever you give me, I'll appreciate."

Dale woke before dawn on Christmas morning. His mom had warned him to stay in bed until at least seven, but the minutes had dragged on. Finally, Dale couldn't stand the suspense. Sliding past his mother's and grandparent's rooms, Dale crept down the stairs, avoiding the squeaks so he wouldn't wake anyone. He made his way to the landing without detection and peered over the railing. The tree in the front living room window stood in silvery glory, illuminated by the moon. Leaning against the branches was the most beautiful present he had ever seen: a ten-foot-long wooden toboggan.

His heart pounded as he ran down the rest of the stairs, forgetting which ones were squeaky. He went right to the toboggan and caressed the smooth wooden bottom. Without disturbing the other presents, he lifted the toboggan and carried it to the center of the room. There he set it down, jumped on the padded seat and took hold of the rope as he pretended to race down Simpson Hill with P. J. and the gang loaded behind him. Just as he leaned into a turn, he heard a gentle voice. "Is it what you wanted?"

Dale looked up and saw his mother looking down at him from the landing, tying the belt on her robe. Dale leapt up the stairs to give her a big hug.

"It's the best present in the whole world!"

"Did you know that your dad and I bought this toboggan three months ago when he was home? He heard you mention it, and he thought you were old enough for a fast sled," Dale's mother said as she wiped her eyes. "He really wanted to be here to give it to you himself."

Dale gave his mother's hand a squeeze. "I hope he'll be home soon."

The rest of the vacation was glorious. The only way it could have been better would have been if Scout were running beside him, nipping at his boots, as Dale and his friends flew down Simpson Hill.

As the sun began to set on the last day of vacation, Dale trudged toward home, red-cheeked and covered with a fine layer of ground-in snow. One by one, porch lights turned on, and he could see a warm glow coming from his own house.

His mother had hot chocolate ready for him as he entered the back door and removed his snowy coat and boots. He slid into his seat and noticed two letters addressed to him were at his place. Noting the official-looking envelope, Dale opened that one first and began reading.

```
TO: Dale Kingston


We are sorry to inform you that your
dog has escaped from the training
facility at Fort Robinson, Nebraska.


        Scout Kingston
        SERIAL NUMBER C4602
        (Border Collie)


                Captain
                Stonemiller
```

"What do they mean, "Escaped?" There must be some mistake!" Dale handed his mom the letter, "Scout wouldn't do that!"

Dale's mom scanned the brief letter from the commanding officer. "I think this letter looks official…"

"It's not Scout. It's some other dog," Dale said, and he pounded this fist on the table. Then he noticed the other letter addressed to him in familiar handwriting. The return address was also from Fort Robinson, from an A. Klimza.

"Mom, this other letter is from Artie! He's going to tell me there's been a mix-up! He's going to tell me that Scout's safe and is the best dog the Army's ever had." Dale tore open the letter and read.

Dear Dale,

I wish I never had to tell you this, but Scout has run off. I tried to be the best handler I could, but one day he escaped through a hole in the fence around the base.

I can't begin to tell you how sorry I am. If there was anything I could do to change things, I would.

I know how much you loved that dog, because I did, too. I'll never give up looking for Scout.

Sincerely,
Artie

Tears dripped softly on the stationary as Dale realized the meaning of Artie's letter. If Artie said so, Scout must really be gone. But that didn't mean he had to accept it. As Dale sat at the table, his mother's arm around his shoulder, he decided he would not let this matter die. Just as Artie had done the week before, Dale vowed that he would do everything he could to locate his missing dog.

Chapter 19

# DEAR MR· PRESIDENT

That evening the conversation at supper was subdued. Dale pushed the noodles around his plate as he thought about Scout. Usually he gobbled up his dinner as he described the day's events, but that night he had lost all interest in what he had done earlier that day. The only thing he could think of was his runaway dog.

After dinner he sat quietly at the table while his mother and grandmother cleared the dishes. His grandfather finally put his arm on Dale's shoulder. "Come on in the living room with me. The President is going to speak tonight. Maybe that will take your mind off Scout for a little bit."

Dale didn't answer; he just got up and followed his grandfather into the living room. Grandpa turned on the

Philco radio so they could listen to President Roosevelt's fireside chat in which he often talked to the American people about the developments of the war. Usually Mr. Roosevelt tried to be upbeat and rally the people behind the war effort. Mom, Grandma and Grandpa sat in their chairs on either side of the radio as Dale stretched out on the floor beneath the speaker, his head resting on the rug in the center of the room. Slowly he traced the flowered pattern on the rug with his fingers.

He usually enjoyed listening to the President's steady, strong voice. This evening, however, Dale couldn't concentrate. The President's words were just a steady drone in the background while his mind turned over the events of the day. *What would Mr. Roosevelt do if he knew Scout were missing? If anyone could help Scout,* Dale reasoned, *the President could. Why not go right to the top?* For the first time since he'd heard the news about Scout, he felt hopeful. He would write a letter to the President, to Mr. Roosevelt himself. With the resources of the United States Army, Scout surely would be found.

While the family listened, Dale excused himself and ran to his room. Grabbing a pen and some paper, he settled himself at his desk.

"Dear Mr. President," he wrote at the top of the page. Carefully he composed a short letter asking for any type of help in finding his dog. Dale added how he had volunteered his dog for Dogs for Defense to help the war effort, but that now his dog was lost.

He signed the letter, folded the paper, and inserted it in an envelope which he addressed to:

PRESIDENT ROOSEVELT
THE WHITE HOUSE
WASHINGTON, D.C.

He tiptoed into his grandfather's room and got a stamp from his desk drawer without being heard. Licking the stamp and placing it in the upper right corner, he decided to mail it on his way to school the next day. He would tell no one about the letter and vowed that nothing would stop him from getting Scout back.

Chapter 20

# WINTER RAGES ON

Dale sat in the kitchen drinking coffee with his grandfather the next morning.

"My, you're up early," his mother said as she entered. "Tell me, where did you disappear to last night during the broadcast?"

"I was tired and thinking about Scout, so I went to bed early."

Grandpa looked up from his paper. "How are you feeling about Scout today?"

"Better. I think we'll find him."

"What do you mean, 'we'?"

"Ah, I mean, they."

Mother sat down. "I sure hope so. Want me to drive you to school since you can't ride your bike?"

"No," Dale said, "I'm meeting P.J. at the fire station. We'll warm up there before finishing the walk to school." He gulped the rest of his coffee, finished his toast, and stood. "I've got to go. I don't want to be late for band."

He ran to the front door past Grandma as she entered. "Be sure to wear a hat, and see you at dinner," she said as he slammed the front door.

Dale watched his breath form white clouds as he walked down Simpson Hill. He was glad he put the letter to the President in his knapsack the night before. Snow crunched under his boots as he worked his way to the Post Office, just before the fire station. *If I hurry*, Dale thought, *I can mail the letter before P.J. sees me.*

The streets were deserted as he neared the Post Office. No one was out this early, so his secret was safe. He raced up the steps of the Post Office and opened the stately glass and metal doors. Breathing a sigh of relief that he had made it without being seen, Dale entered the building, his boots making squeaking sounds on the polished granite floor. Just as he took off his knapsack to take out the letter, he heard a door open behind him and a cheery voice say, "Good morning, Dale. I was sorting mail for my route when I thought I heard someone come in. What are you doing here so early?"

Dale froze and did not know what to say as he stood with the letter in his hand.

"Cat got your tongue?" Mr. Duckhorn said as he walked up to the boy.

Realizing he hadn't answered, Dale said, "I just wanted to mail this before going to the firehouse to pick up P. J."

"You didn't have to come all this way, especially with all this snow. You could've left it for me in the mail box at your home," the mailman said, then walked up to Dale with an outstretched hand. "Let me take it inside for you."

"Don't worry. I'll take care of it," Dale said, but Mr. Duckhorn was too fast. He whisked the letter out of Dale's hand and looked at the envelope.

"Is this a letter to the real President? President Roosevelt?"

"Please, Mr. Duckhorn! Don't tell anyone. It's a secret."

The mailman was silent for a moment before he reassured Dale and shook his hand. "OK, we've got ourselves a secret. I'll personally make sure this letter goes out on the first mail train and that no one inside this office sees it. We don't see many letters addressed to

the White House come through here," he said. "It's our
secret. And as soon as you get a response from the White
House, I'll personally make sure I deliver it to you."

"Thanks, Mr. Duckhorn!" Dale said as he opened
the massive doors and was greeted by a blast of cold air.
Looking down the street to make sure that P. J. wasn't
around, he hurried down the steps and across the street.
As he ran toward the station, P. J. opened the door and
Smokey burst out.

The dog raced in circles, leaping through snow drifts.
Once he found the right spot, he rolled over on his back
and wiggled in the snow. "Get back inside!" P.J. said as he
took hold of Smokey's collar, dragging him back inside.
He couldn't help but think of how much Scout would
have enjoyed playing in the snow with Smokey.

As the two friends walked through the frozen streets
to school, they whipped chunks of snow at trees. By
the time they reached the Emerson School, other band
students were arriving. They shared stories of presents,
sledding, and what they did during their vacation.

Bridget and Chrissy spied Dale as he and P. J. entered
the auditorium. Chrissy said, "I saw you leave your house
really early today. What was that about?"

"Nothing. I just wanted to meet P.J and be sure we

were on time to band," Dale said as he took out his cornet. "I've missed band and all my friends."

"Same here," Bridget said. She turned to talk to Karl and Bobby whom she had not seen since vacation began.

Finally, Mr. Jeffrey stepped on the podium, and everyone quieted down. "I'm glad to see that everyone could get here in the snow. From your conversations, I can tell that you had a great vacation," he said before changing the subject. "Since we just had a concert before the break, I want to change things up a little bit. Your musical abilities have really grown over the past few weeks, and I feel that you're now ready to play solos. I'll also put you in small ensembles of two to five instruments. It's a good way to understand how to balance your parts, and you can see what fun it is to play in a smaller group."

Mr. Jeffrey went onto explain the new schedule. Instead of having band three times a week, they would have band one day, a group lesson another day, and then Mr. Jeffrey would work with each ensemble on another day. The ensembles would also be expected to practice outside of school. The director added, "Since this winter is so cold, it will give you something to do."

Victor said, "When do we find out who we'll be playing with?"

"I'll put up the list at the end of the rehearsal. Now let's get back to playing. It's been a long time."

The band played unison exercises and scales. Then for the last twenty minutes, they worked on a new piece, "I Love you Truly," that Mr. Jeffrey said would be fun to learn for Valentine's Day.

At the end of rehearsal, Mr. Jeffrey invited everyone to view the solo and ensemble list on the back table after instruments had been put away and the stage cleared.

The stage was cleaned twice as fast as usual so that everyone could crowd around the list.

While he waited, Dale glanced out the windows at the dark gray clouds. Snow was gusting in swirls off the roof, and he could barely see the flagpole that was just outside the window.

Victor said, "We're going to have a tough time getting home today."

Dale didn't answer. He was thinking about Scout. *Would he be able to survive weather like this on the windy plains of Nebraska?* He felt a shiver go up his spine as a big gust of wind whipped more snow in front of the windows.

P. J. poked him in the back. "Dale, get over here."

Eight hundred miles to the west, Nebraska was having

one of the worst winters on record. Cold winds swept across the prairie, creating ground blizzards so intense that Artie could hardly see the kennels from his barracks. He scratched a hole in the frost on the window and peered out, but it was so dark that he could see nothing but swirling snowflakes.

*How could a dog survive in weather like this?* Artie thought as he threw another log into the stove. When he was young, Artie had a dog on his Montana ranch that had suffered frostbite on the pads of his paws from being out in the cold too long. He remembered nursing the tender, cracked paws gently back to health. It took weeks before the dog could stand, and from then on, his paws were always sensitive to cold weather.

Artie slipped his winter parka over his sweater and pulled the fur-lined hood over his head. He carried several dog leashes he had repaired with him as he headed for the kennel. The snowfall had been so great that the Army had put ropes up between the buildings for the soldiers to hold onto. Several times soldiers had gotten lost in ground blizzards and had to be rescued or they might have frozen to death.

Artie opened the barracks door and icy pellets stung his face as he grabbed the rope that led to the kennels.

With his head tucked down, he worked his way down the rope. About halfway, he stopped and listened. *What was that sound?* he thought as he stood clinging to the rope in the roaring wind.

Then he heard it again. *What's that? Was that a voice?* He remained still and listened. After several minutes he decided it must have been the wind, so he continued down the rope. For a brief minute the wind subsided, and then he heard it again. This time, he heard a faint voice calling, "Help me! Is anyone out there to help me?" Artie turned in the direction of the voice, but he could not see anyone, he only heard the voice, saying, "Help me, please!"

As Artie shielded his eyes from the blinding snow, he realized the voice was familiar. "Joe? Joe, is that you?"

Artie waited for an answer, but he heard nothing. Then, just above the whine of the wind, he heard, "Help me!"

Artie could tell Joe was close, but he still could not see him. By the sound of the voice, he could tell his friend was off to his right, but where? He thought about what to do. "Joe, it's me, Artie. Hold on, I'm coming. Can you keep calling?" At first he heard nothing. He was about to panic when finally he heard a response. "Hurry, Artie, I'm freezing."

Joe's voice continued as Artie put a plan into action. He had eight leashes with clips on one end and handles on the other. He hooked the first clip onto the guide rope and then hooked each leash onto the other until all eight were a continuous line. If Joe were farther away than that, he wouldn't be able to get him, which would mean certain death. Once the leashes were hooked together, Artie slowly left the guide rope, holding on to the leashes as he walked head first into the ground blizzard, the snow cutting at his face. When he reached the end of the eighth leash he stopped and yelled. "Where are you?"

Off to his right, Artie heard, "Over here, over here." In the blinding snow, he could not judge how far away Joe was, so he began inching forward, holding onto the final leash as far as he could. When he thought he could go no farther, he tripped over something on the ground. It was Joe lying in the snow.

Artie kept one hand on the leash and used his other arm to help his buddy to his feet. The two struggled back to the guide rope. When they arrived at the rope, Artie tied the leashes around Joe's waist so he wouldn't lose him on the way back to the barracks.

At the entrance to the barracks, Artie kicked open the door and dragged Joe inside. One soldier ran over with some blankets while another slammed the door closed against the raging storm.

Joe lay on the bunk shivering with the dog leashes still tied around his waist.

"I thought we were both going to die," Artie said as he unclipped the leashes from his friend's waist. After he undid the final leash, he stopped and held it in his hands, not saying a word. "I think you can thank Scout for saving your life tonight. The eighth leash, the last one... without that leash, I wouldn't have been able to reach you. That was Scout's old leash, the one I'd just repaired."

Joe held the leash with his shaking hand. "Artie, we've got to find that dog," he gasped. "I can't bear the thought of him alone in this weather."

Chapter 21

## AN OFFER OF HELP

Four weeks had passed since Dale mailed his letter to the President. Every day he checked to see if the mailman had made his delivery, but no response arrived. Playing his instrument helped to take Dale's mind off of the letter. He was playing in a brass quintet with Sandra on trumpet, Victor on French horn, Karl on trombone, and P. J. on tuba. He also was assigned a cornet solo, "A Soldier's Dream," by Walter B. Rogers. Dale was drawn to the title immediately, and he thanked Mr. Jeffrey for selecting the solo for him.

Valentine's Day was just around the corner, as was Dale's birthday. The coming birthday wasn't just an ordinary one—it would be his twelfth, which was a special occasion in the Kingston household. His parents promised him that when he turned twelve, he would be old enough and responsible enough to have additional privileges. His parents didn't say exactly what they would allow him to do, but knowing all the things he couldn't do, he had hope that he would be able to add some of them to the list of new privileges.

During the past four weeks, the quintet met with Mr. Jeffrey three times and had practiced at both Sandra's and Dale's homes three times. Now it was Friday, and the group was to meet with Mr. Jeffrey for the fourth time. They were anxious to play the song straight through for their director.

Victor was waiting at the door of the auditorium for Dale. "Do you think we're ready?"

"I think so, considering how we played at Sandra's house after school. Come on, let's go warm up.

The boys took out their instruments and began playing long tones. Soon Karl and Sandra joined them.

After they had thoroughly warmed up, Mr. Jeffrey, who had been looking through scores at the back table, walked over to the group. "Today is the deadline for playing straight through the piece. I'm looking forward to it, but where is P. J.?"

At that exact moment P. J. burst through the door with

his shirt hanging out, sweat beading up on his forehead. "Sorry I'm late. I forgot both my mouthpiece and my music and had to run home after I was halfway here."

Mr. Jeffrey smiled. "Well, I'm glad you made it. Catch your breath and get your tuba out. We're ready to start."

P. J. hurried to his seat. Mr. Jeffrey had taught them that in brass ensembles, the first cornet or trumpet part is the lead. All of the players should watch the leader as he nods his head as a cue for the starting tempo. In this song, Dale was playing first cornet. He told Sandra that on the next song, she could play first so that she would have a chance to lead the group.

"May we tune first?" Dale said. "Tuning helps our balance and blend."

Dale walked over to the piano and played a low B-flat. P. J. held out his B-flat, but stopped because the pitches did not match. "Sharp," P. J. said, and he pulled out one of his slides. "OK, play it again."

Dale played the note again, and this time P. J. was satisfied. Karl played next, holding his trombone slide in first position, followed by Victor, who played an F on his horn. After Sandra tuned, Dale had her play her note again and he tuned his cornet to her. After several adjustments, Dale said, "I think we're ready."

"Go right ahead. I'll watch your parts on my score and check for mistakes."

Dale looked at each player to make sure they were paying attention. Then he bobbed his head three times, and on the fourth nod, everyone took a breath together, and the ensemble began to play.

At the end of the piece, they looked up at Mr. Jeffrey expectantly. The director sat in his chair staring at the score.

"What's wrong Mr. Jeffrey?" Victor said. "Did we do something wrong?"

He looked up and clapped his hands. "Bravo! I've been listening to ensembles these past two days, and you're by far the best. You played like you've been together for years. I'll keep this group together from now until you graduate from high school. I see a state championship in your future."

P. J. said, "So you thought it was good?"

Everyone laughed. "It was not only good, it was fantastic."

For the next twenty minutes Mr. Jeffrey worked on dynamics with them, and notes on a few of the more intricate sections. At the end of the rehearsal he wished them a good weekend. "Keep having fun playing together. Your practice time has really paid off."

The rest of the day was full of assignments and tests, followed by an art project at the end of the day: decorating a shoebox for Valentine's Day. All the boxes had to have a slit in the top so that others could put valentines into them.

Bridget came up to Dale and peered over his shoulder. "I really like the way you decorated your box this year."

"Thanks, I like yours, too. I'll have to finish making my valentines. What about you?"

Bridget smiled. "Mine are all done."

"Well, I guess I know what I'm doing this weekend," Dale said as Bridget turned and flipped her ponytail off her shoulder as she returned to her desk.

Dale placed his finished box on the shelf with the others and cleaned up his art supplies.

Before the students left for the day, Mrs. Johnstone, the art teacher, said, "On Monday morning the room will be open before school so you may come and pick up your finished box and put it in Mrs. Cooper's room for Valentine's Day. Remember, you must have a valentine for each student in your class." She shooed the students back to class before the dismissal bell rang.

Everyone was loaded down with books and instruments to take home for the weekend. Dale and his friends had to walk home through the snow that seemed to linger. The walk went quickly as they threw snowballs at every tree and at each other. One by one, the boys dropped off at each of their homes until only P. J. and Dale were left. When they got to the firehouse, P. J. ran inside to greet Smokey, and Dale began the walk up Main Street to Simpson Hill. As he passed the alley next to the Post Office, he heard a voice call, "Dale, I think your letter has arrived!"

At first Dale could not figure out where the voice was coming from; then he spotted Mr. Duckhorn waving to him. Dale quickly looked back to see if P. J. was around, then ducked into the alley.

Mr. Duckhorn waved the letter in his hand. Dale took the envelope with The White House return address in the upper-left-hand corner. He stared at his name, typed in bold letters in the center.

"Go ahead and open it," Mr. Duckhorn urged as he leaned over Dale's shoulder. "I've never seen a letter from the White House before."

Dale opened the envelope carefully so he would not rip the letter. In a shaky voice, he read...

Dear Dale,

On behalf of the United States Military and the Dogs for Defense program, I am extremely sorry to hear about the loss of your dog, Scout. I have sent a notice to Commanding Officer Sheffield at Fort Robinson, Nebraska, asking him to do everything within his power to see that Scout is found. Until then, please accept these dog tags with Scout's name and serial number embossed on them.

Without the sacrifices of citizens such as you for the war effort, we would not be making the advances we have made recently.

Sincerely,
Franklin D. Roosevelt
FDR

P.S. If this letter gets to you in time, please listen to my radio program on Friday, February 9, 1945, at 7:00 p.m.

Dale and the mailman stood silently in the cold afternoon air. The President had actually written him a letter and had promised that the military would look for Scout. Dale tipped the envelope upside down, and a chain with two rectangular metal objects spilled out into his glove. He held the tags up to Mr. Duckhorn, who admired the indented letters in neat rows.

"Today is February ninth. Why would the President want you to listen tonight?"

"I don't know, but let's promise not to tell anybody. We'll just go home and listen. We'll both find out in a few hours."

Mr. Duckhorn agreed as Dale put the letter and dog tags back in the envelope. As he hid the letter deep in his knapsack, Mr. Duckhorn said, "I wish I could see the faces on your family tonight when they hear the President talk and then you show them the letter."

Dale was filled with energy. "Thanks," he said as he took off running.

Chapter 22

# THE SECRET IS OUT

Dale burst through the back door and slid to a stop on the kitchen's linoleum floor.

"Whoa! What's the hurry?" Grandma said as she opened the oven. "Close that door before all the heat gets out of the house, young man, and next time, slow down."

"Sorry. When's dinner? And will Mom and Grandpa be here tonight?"

"We're having fried chicken, baked potatoes, and some canned green beans from last year's garden. How does that sound?"

Dale thought that sounded fine and ran upstairs to his room. "Call me when it's ready."

He closed the door so no one would see the letter. He sat on the bed and read it over, still not believing that the President of the United States had written to him. Dale took the dog tags out of the envelope and put them around his neck, feeling the embossed lettering on the tags. *Maybe, just maybe, they'll find Scout.*

Dale lay back on his bed. He wondered if Scout had survived the winter and where he might be. When he heard his mom call, "Dale, dinner is ready," he realized he must have fallen asleep.

Startled, he jumped up and ran down the stairs two at a time and slid into his seat.

"You must be one hungry young man to move like that," his mother said. "Why don't you start the chicken first?"

Dale took some chicken and passed the plate to his grandfather, who was watching him carefully.

"You seem really wound up. What happened today to get you all fired up?"

"Nothing," Dale said as he plunged his fork into his potatoes. "I guess I'm excited about Valentine's Day and my birthday coming up." Then, so as not to arouse suspicion, he said, "After dinner are we going to listen to the President on the radio?"

Mother raised her eyebrows. "How did you know the President was speaking tonight?"

"Oh, I heard Mrs. Cooper talking about it today and thought maybe we could listen tonight."

"Hmmm, I don't know. I've got some work to get done before the morning," she said, but when Grandpa looked at her questioningly, she relented and said, "but we can sit with you if you want."

Dale had to control his excitement to keep from drawing attention to himself. He talked about how well the ensemble had played and what Mr. Jeffrey told them. After dinner Grandma was surprised that Dale offered to help with the dishes. He didn't want her to miss the President's talk.

At six fifty-five Grandpa turned on the radio and dialed in the station. After several turns, the static disappeared, and the announcer said, "Good evening and welcome to a fireside chat with Franklin Delano Roosevelt." Dale lay on the floor as usual with Grandma and Grandpa on one side and his mom on the other.

In a strong voice, the President opened, "Good evening from the White House. I'd like to start tonight's program with a letter I recently received from a young man in Libertyville, Indiana."

Grandfather's ears perked up. "Did he say Libertyville?"

"Hush up! We can't hear," Grandmother said.

## "Let me read it to you," the President continued.

Dear Mr. President,

My name is Dale Kingston, and I volunteered my dog, a black-and-white Border Collie named Scout to the Dogs for Defense program at Fort Robinson, Nebraska, back in November.

I felt I needed to do my part as a citizen to help in the war effort.

Unfortunately, I recently received a letter telling me that Scout had escaped, and no one in the military could find him. I am very worried about him now that winter is here.

Can you help me find my dog?

I understand you are busy, but I can't give up hope. Thanks for anything you can do to help.

Sincerely,
Dale Kingston
Libertyville, Indiana

The President paused for a moment before continuing.

Dale glanced first at his mother, then his grandmother and grandfather. They were sitting with their mouths wide open staring at the radio, saying nothing.

"Let me continue to explain why I am sharing this letter with the nation and the soldiers around the world. It's because of citizens like young Dale that our country will always rise to any challenge. I hope all Americans will continue to help as we try to end the war against tyranny. I've sent an executive order to the commander at Fort Robinson to do whatever it takes to find Scout and return him to Dale. I personally sent Dale a letter stating my intentions. If any American sees this black-and-white Border Collie with the serial number C4602 tattooed on its left ear and belly, please contact Fort Robinson immediately. And Dale, if you are listening, thank you from the bottom of my heart for selflessly volunteering your dog for the good of the nation."

The President closed by urging the audience to buy war bonds to support the military effort. When he finished, Grandpa leaned over and turned off the radio as the family sat in silence.

Concerned, Dale said, "I would've asked you if I could

write the letter, but I was afraid that you'd think it was silly." Dale took the letter out of his pocket and held it out to Grandpa.

Grandpa examined the letter carefully, shook his head and said, "I'm so proud of you for taking the initiative to write the President. I don't know what to say." Then Dale's mom spoke as she wiped tears from her eyes. "Come here and give me a hug."

As Dale leaned over to hug his mom, he said, "He even sent me dog tags with Scout's name."

Grandpa fingered the tags around Dale's neck. "Well, I'll be darned. You not only got a letter from the President, but he mentioned your name to the entire nation and all the troops around the world. If he can't help find Scout, no one can."

That same evening, eight hundred miles to the west, Artie and Joe sat on their bunks in front of the radio as they listened to the President's broadcast. They both looked at each other in disbelief when the President mentioned Scout and his owner, Dale Kingston. They knew that Commander Sheffield would be sending orders to find that dog, and they were ready to help.

Three thousand miles farther west, on a small island in the South Pacific, Dale's father, Jake, and his fellow soldiers were resting in their tent, listening to the radio. His buddies wanted to know if Dale Kingston was related to him. "Aren't you from Libertyville, Jake?" Dale's father leaned back and said, "Yes, I am, and he's my son." At the end of the broadcast, Jake got out some paper to write a letter to Dale.

Chapter 23

# SPRING THAW

It had been almost three weeks since the President had talked about Dale and Scout on the radio. In the days and weeks after the broadcast, people Dale didn't even know congratulated him. Mrs. Foster, an elderly lady who lived down the street, said she was praying for Scout's safe return. Mrs. Johnstone had her elementary art students draw pictures of the dog and make posters urging people with the phrase Bring Scout Home in bold letters. Students hung them in the school and store windows of Libertyville.

During school announcements, Principal Prenty thanked Dale for his outstanding citizenship and his positive contribution as a member of the Emerson School student body. Bridget and Chrissy made Scout a valentine box as if he were a member of the class so that everyone could send him cards. Bridget even included a dog biscuit in her valentine to Scout.

One evening after the Kingston family finished dinner, General Packston called to commend Dale for his sacrifice toward the war effort. He expressed gratitude that he had donated Scout to such a worthy program. He added that with the full power of the military behind the search, he was confident that Scout would be found.

But the best time of all had been at his twelfth birthday. The party was at P. J.'s house, and all of the gang was included, even Chrissy, Bridget and Sandra. Once the girls left, Mr. Walsh, P. J.'s dad, drove the boys to the fire station so they could spend the night playing there. They brought their sleeping bags, snacks, and even got to drink all the pop they wanted out of the cooler. Mr. Walsh showed the boys how to slide down the brass fire pole that went from the second to the first floor. He warned the boys, "Be sure to wrap your arms and legs around the pole as you slide down. The tighter you hold on, the slower you'll go and the looser you hold on the faster you'll go."

Mr. Walsh also showed the boys how to put on the boots, coats, and hats that were lined up on the wall.

"Once you slide down from the second floor, you can practice getting dressed and getting into the trucks. I'll time you."

Finally, in the wee hours of the morning, they collapsed in their sleeping bags. Some of the boys slept in the back of the fire truck, others in the cab, and a few even went up on the roof to sleep under the stars despite the coolness of the night. Dale's legs ached the next morning after running up the stairs to the second floor and sliding down the pole, pretending they were going to a fire.

The events of the past three weeks whirred through Dale's mind as he rode to school. There was still a little nip in the spring air, but the early morning sun warmed it up by the time school let out. The gang decided they should check out the fort in the Jungle to see what damage the long hard winter had done. They planned to clean up the fort so that it was ready for a spring and summer of war games.

Dale had called each of his friends the night before and told them to meet at the fire station at seven-thirty sharp that morning so they could ride to band together. He had missed the morning rides and the fun they had on the way to school. As he coasted down Simpson Hill, the breeze in his hair, he thought about Scout. He received a letter from Commanding Officer Sheffield, explaining that his men were doing everything possible to find the dog. He promised to keep Dale informed of any new developments. Yesterday, the best letter had arrived: one from his dad. He relayed how he had heard the President's talk. He wanted Dale to know how proud he was of him and how he hoped he would be home soon. As Dale read the letter alone in his bedroom, he wiped his eyes. He wished that the war would end quickly so his dad could come home safely. If Scout were found, they could all be together once again.

At the bottom of Simpson Hill, Dale's thoughts were interrupted when his friends darted out from an alley, surprising him and almost causing him to wreck his bike. He slid to a stop so as not to hit them. "You scared me half to death!"

Tommy laughed. "That's why we did it. We knew you'd be daydreaming, so we planned an ambush. We're just practicing for the Jungle."

"Well you'd better keep practicing. You haven't won a game of Capture the Flag yet," Dale said. "Let's race. We haven't done that in a while," then took off on his bike.

P. J. anticipated the race and had a head start, but the rest of the boys were in hot pursuit. Dale stood up as he pedaled furiously, the bikes swerving back and forth through the streets of Libertyville.

As P. J. skidded to a stop at the bike rack, Victor said, "No fair. P. J. cheated."

Bobby, Dave, Karl, and Dale all tried to outdo one another's skid marks as they pulled up to the bike rack.

Victor was the last to slide his tires on the pavement. "Finally we have tire marks on the sidewalk, a real sign of spring."

P. J., the sweat running down the side of his face, examined the sidewalk. "I agree, but mine's the best."

"A cheater like you would make the biggest marks," Karl said as he grabbed his trombone and ran to the school so he wouldn't be late for band.

Mr. Jeffrey had selected new music for the spring concert. Chrissy was to play a flute solo, so the band was learning how to accompany a soloist. They had to play soft enough for her flute to be heard, while at the same time maintaining excitement and dynamics in the music. Mr. Jeffrey said, "If this solo goes well, other students can volunteer to play solos for the next concert." Sandra leaned over to Dale and said, "Why don't you volunteer?"

Once the chairs and stands were set up and instruments tuned, Mr. Jeffrey stepped on the podium and began the rehearsal with the daily warm-up from their chorale book. That morning he chose "Faith of our Fathers" by Frederick Faber. Dale was familiar with the chorale because it was a hymn they sang in church on Sundays.

As the band began to play, Dale stopped and listened as the music filled the auditorium. Sunlight streamed through the windows, and he felt apprehensive. He couldn't help thinking of Scout. Where was he? Why hadn't he heard anything?

Chapter 24

## ARTIE'S LEAVE

By the time the spring thaw had arrived, Artie was so grateful for warm weather that he didn't mind sloshing through deep mud on his way to the kennels. He had been assigned a new dog named King, a highly intelligent German shepherd. But the soldier missed the special relationship he had developed with Scout. No dog would take Scout's place as far as Artie was concerned.

Ever since Scout's escape, Artie had not been the same. He had lost nearly ten pounds from his already thin frame. Each time he went to town on leave, he found his eyes scanning the countryside for signs of Scout. A movement in the grass here, a flash of fur there would raise his hopes, which were dashed moments later when a cat or some other small animal emerged from tall grass along the side of the road.

Artie had been at Fort Robinson long enough to earn a two-week leave of absence. In early March he decided to return home to Montana. Perhaps being back on the ranch would raise his spirits and help him get back to being his old self. Joe sat on his bunk as Artie packed his duffle bag with a few of his belongings. He watched as his friend carefully folded a shirt and placed it in the bag.

"Joe, when I get to the ranch, all I want to do is sit on the front porch and smell the grass and earth after a good rain. I'm especially looking forward to home-cooked meals. But most of all, I just want to ride my horse Salty with my dog Rex by my side while we herd sheep through the pastures."

"I'm going to miss you, Artie, but I think you need a change of pace."

Artie nodded, and for the first time in months, he began to feel excited. He dressed in a freshly pressed uniform and took a few extra minutes to buff his shoes to a radiant shine. After everything was packed, he cinched the drawstring and slung the duffle bag over his shoulder. Joe offered to drive him to the train depot, where he would catch the train to Rapid City, South Dakota. At Rapid City he would board a train to Billings, Montana, the town closest to his ranch. There his dad would meet him and drive him the final fifty miles home.

Artie waved through the train window to Joe, who was standing beside the jeep. Gradually his bunkmate and the station faded from sight, and the agony of losing Scout seemed to be left behind as he settled into his seat and fell fast asleep. Visions of the ranch entered his dreams as the train steamed through the countryside. When Artie awoke, the scenery had changed from the flat farmlands of Nebraska to the rolling hills of the South Dakota Badlands. Changing trains at Rapid City, he headed northwest toward the familiar territory of his home state.

As the train chugged into Billings, Artie searched through the dusty window for the familiar face of his dad. Artie and his father looked alike. Both had the same tall, thin frame, but his dad's hair was now gray and his face weathered from years of work outdoors on the ranch. On the edge of the platform, Artie spotted his father, standing with his hands in his pockets. He was wearing his good cowboy hat, the one for weddings and special occasions. It was great to be almost home.

Chapter 25

# HERDING SHEEP

Artie whistled his favorite Glenn Miller song, "In the Mood" as the fields whizzed by. He loved riding in the pickup truck, enjoying all the details of the country scenery: telephone poles stretched endlessly, mile after mile along the road; a redwing blackbird perched on a fence post; Burma Shave signs occasionally sprang up to break up the landscape.

Artie felt his energy returning. Although he had been awake for nearly twenty-four hours, he didn't feel the least bit sleepy. He smiled at the familiar rolling mountain lowlands—miles and miles of empty land occupied only by cattle, sheep, and ranches. Artie and his father didn't talk much as the truck rolled down the road. The two of them had an understanding, and though they had been apart many months, his dad knew that Artie needed time to let the magic of being home do its work.

Up ahead they spotted a wrangler on horseback herding sheep across the road. Artie's father pulled the truck to a stop. There was no getting across the road now. Artie figured there had to be at least two thousand of the white, wooly creatures. Three dogs corralled the animals and kept them moving across the road. As soon as a sheep strayed, one of the dogs would tear after it, cut it off, and force it back in the direction of the herd. Artie and his father watched as the dogs ran back and forth, guiding the moving herd. "Billy Jackson raises the best sheep dogs in the country," his Dad said about the rancher who owned the land on both sides of the road.

The sheep moved closer to the truck, and the chorus of bleating increased in volume. A bunch of sheep broke off from the main herd and swept behind the pickup truck. Before Artie and his father knew it, the truck had become an island in the middle of a moving current of sheep. Wave after wave continued streaming around the truck and across the road until the dogs forced the herd back together and away from the pickup.

One dog in particular caught Artie's eye. That dog was a black-and-white Border Collie extremely adept at keeping the sheep in tow. Up and down the edge of the herd the dog raced, nudging any sheep that got out of line back into place.

"Dad, you know in one of my letters I wrote you about a dog that got away…" Artie's voice dropped off as he dismissed the coincidence in his mind as being just too great. He'd been fooled before and chased a Border Collie all over Nebraska for nothing. *There's no way that any dog could have survived a winter out on the plains, especially the kind of winter we've had this year,* he thought. He also knew that the distance from Billings to Fort Robinson was more than five hundred miles. Still, he watched the dog carefully.

The herd finished crossing the road and the sheep spread over the foothill meadows, grazing lazily in the midday sun. The vigilant black-and-white dog continued to patrol the outside edges of the flock. Artie's father started the engine just as the wrangler pulled his horse next to Artie's window.

"Sorry for making you wait such a long time," he apologized. "Mr. Jackson wanted us to get these sheep to the new pasture before noon today." The wrangler, covered with dust, sat atop a handsome chestnut mare.

"Don't worry about it," Artie said, as he continued to stare at the dog. His dad shifted the truck into gear. Artie placed his hand on his father's forearm and leaned out the window to talk to the wrangler. "Those are mighty good dogs you have, sir. That black-and-white one... how long have you had him?

"Him? Oh, he wandered up to the ranch about two months ago. Fit in real well with the rest of the dogs. Learned real quick, too."

Artie's mind was racing. He argued with himself. *Could it possibly be? No, it couldn't...It can't be him... but then again...* Swallowing and taking a deep breath, he said, "Well, sir, I'm with the Army canine unit stationed at Fort Robinson, Nebraska. I worked with a dog that looked just like that dog of yours. Last December he ran away, and we never found him."

Artie's father shifted the truck back into neutral. The wrangler leaned forward in his saddle, "Are you trying to tell me you think this is your dog? No dog could have covered that many miles during the winter." He rubbed his grizzled stubble of chin whiskers. "No, soldier, you're sadly mistaken if you think that's your dog." Picking up the reins of his horse, he said, "'Sides, Mr. Jackson's not going to want to give up a natural-born sheep dog without more proof." With a light tug on the reins, the rancher turned the horse and trotted toward the sheep.

Artie learned against the seat, and his dad shifted back into first gear. He watched as one sheep moved away from the grazing herd toward a small hill of rocks about a hundred yards ahead of the truck. The black-and-white dog's ears perked up, and as the sheep moved farther out of range, the dog barked a warning of several high-pitched yips. Artie sat up, "That bark sounds just like…" and suddenly he knew that he could prove whether or not the dog was Scout.

"Dad, stop the truck!" Artie yelled. The pickup jerked to a halt. He opened the door and sprang to the ground. Waving his long arms, he ran after the man on horseback, "Sir, I can prove that he's my dog… and Dale's."

The wrangler turned and watched as Artie dashed toward him. With a gentle squeeze of his knees, he urged the horse forward until he was looking down at Artie. "I can prove he's AWOL from the Army."

"Now how's that?"

"If that's Scout, he'll have an identification number tattooed inside his left ear," and with that Artie whistled and called Scout's name. The dog lifted his ears and scanned the herd. He ran a few steps and stopped. The wrangler looked down at Artie and drummed his fingers on his saddle. Artie tried again, "Scout, here, boy. C'mon, Scout." The dog jerked his head toward Artie, who leaned down and slapped his thighs. "Scout!"

Instantly the dog's forepaws lifted off the ground, and he raced toward Artie at breakneck speed. Jumping up on Artie, he knocked him onto the dusty road and licked every square inch of his face.

"Well, mister, if he's not your dog, he sure acts like it," the wrangler said as he swung his leg over his saddle and dropped to the ground.

Artie stood up and dusted off his rumpled uniform. He bent down and triumphantly lifted the dog's ear to show the familiar number: C4602. Artie hugged Scout with all his might while the wrangler shook his head in amazement. "Well, I guess we're going to lose one good sheep dog. But if he's an Army dog, at least I know our country is in pretty good hands." Artie shook the man's dusty hand. "Go ahead and take him." Artie opened the door of the pickup and Scout hopped in.

As the truck drove away, Scout stuck his head out the window as if saying goodbye to the sheep. The wrangler was still shaking his head as he watched the pickup disappear in a cloud of dust. "No one's going to believe me when I tell this story at chow tonight."

Chapter 26

## THINGS TO COME

It was the middle of March, and Dale still had no word from the Army. He and Victor leaned against the fort, breathing hard from the last Capture the Flag game. Dale's pants were muddy from crawling through the creek to escape being seen, and his face was coved in dust and sweat. Still, the warm sun felt good on his skin as he rested. Tommy and Bobby had climbed the big oak tree and were sitting on heavy limbs, enjoying the cool breeze. P. J., Dave, and Karl sat on the roof of the fort, basking in the sun like lizards.

"I've been thinking about the next few months," Karl said. "We're going to have some great times."

"Like what?" Tommy said from the tree limb above the roof.

"Well, for starters, how about our first sleepover here at the fort?"

Dale sat up. "And how about our first visit to the junior high and the band auditions?"

P. J. said, "What about our first quintet performance in April?"

Each of the boys began adding different experiences they thought they would have over the coming months until the Conn factory whistle blew, signaling it was time to head home for dinner. They put their helmets back in the fort and closed the door before jumping on their bikes. On the way home, as they chatted about the coming months, P. J. slammed on his brakes and slid to a stop.

"I got it, I got it," he said as the boys turned their bikes around and rode back to where P. J. had stopped.

"You've got what?" Tommy said.

"I think we should give this coming spring and summer a name. Why don't we call it 'A Summer of Fun?'" he suggested.

"That's dumb," Victor said. "I like 'A Summer of New Stuff.'"

"That's no good," Dale said. "How about 'A Summer of Firsts?'"

Karl thought that was the best. "Since we're all twelve, why don't we make a list of twelve new things we've always wanted to do but haven't. Our list could be both firsts for the gang and firsts for ourselves. At the end of the summer, we can see how many each of us accomplished."

The boys leaned on their handlebars for a moment, and finally Bobby said, "You know, this could become something we do for the rest of the time we're together, even in high school."

"Wait. I'm not even out of grade school yet," Dave moaned.

"Bobby is right. We'll all be doing new things in the years to come." As Dale spoke, the boys formed a circle with their bikes in the middle of the deserted street. "Let's take a vote. All in favor of making a list raise your hand." All of the boys raised their hands. "Now, all in favor of naming this summer 'A Summer of Firsts,' raise your hand." Again, each one raised his hand.

P. J. moved his bike out of the circle. "Let's get home. I'm hungry, and I want to get started on my list."

The boys parted ways. Dale quickly pedaled the remaining blocks to his house. As he rounded the top of the hill, he noticed his mother on the front porch waving something in her hand. He slid to a stop on the grass in the front yard, jumped off his bike, and leapt up the stairs of the porch.

"It's a telegram for you!" Dale grabbed it, ripped it open, and began reading.

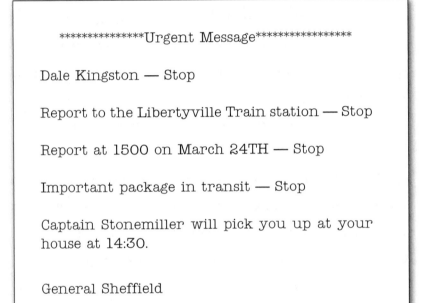

***************Urgent Message****************

Dale Kingston — Stop

Report to the Libertyville Train station — Stop

Report at 1500 on March 24TH — Stop

Important package in transit — Stop

Captain Stonemiller will pick you up at your house at 14:30.

General Sheffield

Dale sat down on the steps and handed the telegram to his mother. She furrowed her brow as she read.

"What do you think this means?" she said.

Dale shook his head. "March 24th. That's tomorrow."

Chapter 27

# BOXCAR FULL OF SURPRISES

Captain Stonemiller's jeep roared down the street at precisely fourteen hundred and thirty hours. Dale had been waiting on the steps of the porch for over an hour in case he came early.

"Bye, Mom," Dale said as he raced down the steps. He jumped in the front seat and heard the soft jingle of the dog tags he had put on for good luck.

"Good to see you again," Captain Stonemiller said over the rumble of the engine.

Dale's mother followed him to the jeep and asked, "Captain, what's this all about?"

"Sorry, ma'am. I'm only following orders. I have no information other than to take Dale to meet the eastbound number eighteen train at fifteen hundred hours today."

With a quick salute, the captain peeled the jeep around and took off down Simpson Hill.

Captain Stonemiller pulled into the parking lot reserved for military personnel. Dale followed as he wound his way through the crowded station. Dale could not believe all of the people sitting in the rows and rows of wooden benches, laughing, crying, and saying goodbye to loved ones going off to war. He glanced up at the giant clock at the end of the waiting area. It read fourteen-fifty-five.

In the yard, train engines were steaming, their brakes hissing. Eastbound number eighteen had just pulled in. The many doors opened, and people began streaming out. Dale watched intently, but he was not sure who or what he was looking for. Finally the last person departed the train. Dale looked at Captain Stonemiller.

"Sorry, son. I'm not sure what or who we're looking for."

Then Dale saw a conductor he had met on one of his trips to Chicago with his grandfather.

"Excuse me, Mr. Paulson," Dale said as he walked up to gray-haired man in a blue uniform.

"Hi, Dale, how's your grandfather?" Mr. Paulson said as he looked over Dale's shoulder. "Is he here with you?"

"No. Captain Stonemiller and I were told to report to this train," Dale continued as he scanned the train for something familiar. "Has everyone gotten off the train?"

The conductor nodded. "We're getting ready to board the next passengers any minute now." Dale lowered his head and fingered the dog tags around his neck. The brakes of the train on the next track let out a long hiss that startled Dale. Mr. Paulson turned and looked down the length of the train. "Wait a minute. Why don't you check the last car, the boxcar?" and he waved his hand down the track. "I heard we had some very special cargo in there," he said as he looked at Captain Stonemiller. "Run down there and ask the freight engineer."

"Thanks," Dale said as he ran down the platform to the boxcar. He arrived at the last car just as a freight engineer was opening the large wooden door on the side.

Dale ran up to the man. "Sir, are you going to unload this car now?"

The engineer nodded and glanced at the captain's military uniform. "We have some express cargo for a Captain Stonemiller, and," he said as he looked down at the clipboard in his hands, "a Dale Kingston." He extended his hand. "I'm guessing you're Captain Stonemiller and you must be Dale." He pumped both the captain and Dale's hands. "Give me a minute. We'll have this door open in a jiffy."

Dale heart began to race as the door scraped back. When it was fully opened, Dale stepped up to peer inside the shadowy train car. With one hand on the door, he leaned in for a better look, only to have an object fly at him from somewhere inside the car. Before he could get out of the way, he was knocked to the ground. A rough, wet tongue began licking him. After the shock of the tackle, he realized Scout was standing on his chest. With both arms, he clutched the dog and held him tightly to his chest.

"I knew you would come back to me! I knew you would!" Dale nestled his head against the dog's fur, running his fingers through his coarse mane. Then a shadow passed over the boy and his dog. Dale squinted up at the figure that was standing above him in the bright sunlight. The person was holding a leash.

"I wouldn't have missed this moment for anything," the dark figure said.

Dale thought, *I know that voice.* He pushed Scout off his chest and stood up. As the figure came into focus, he realized the voice was that of his father, who was smiling at him, Scout's leash in one hand and a duffle bag over his shoulder.

Dale's dad dropped his gear, and Dale fell into his arms. Father and son embraced as Scout circled anxiously and barked.

Captain Stonemiller shifted from foot to foot before interrupting, "Sir, I'll take your bag and drive you both home."

Dad nodded and grabbed the leash. "Lead the way."

Captain Stonemiller turned and led the two, Dale holding his father's hand tightly while Scout trotted behind them.

"Your mom will be surprised to see us both, don't you think?"

Dale agreed. His "Summer of Firsts" had just begun.

# ABOUT THE AUTHORS

Paul Kimpton grew up in a musical family and was a band director in Illinois for thirty-four years. His father, Dale, was a high school band director and professor at the University of Illinois, and his mother, Barbara, was a vocalist. When Paul is not writing, he is reading or enjoying the outdoors.

Ann Kimpton played French horn through college and went on to be a mother, teacher, and high school administrator. Her parents, Henry and Maryalyce Kaczkowski, both educators, instilled an appreciation of the fine arts and the outdoors in all of their children.

Ann and Paul were high school sweethearts who met when they played together in high school band. They have two grown children, Inga and Aaron, who share their love of music, the outdoors, and adventure, and a grandson, Henry, who will continue the tradition.

Also available in the *Adventure with Music* series:

Book 1
## Starting Early

Coming soon
in the *Adventures with Music* series

Book 3

# A Summer of Firsts

As Dale and his friends climbed the steps to the junior high, a tall dark-haired boy stepped in front of them. Dale looked up and said, "Can you tell us where the band room is?"

The boy smirked and looked over at his friends who were leaning against the railing. "Hey, aren't you that hot shot cornet player from Emerson School, the one who saved the town from the fire." The boy stared down at Dale, his feet planted firmly on the ground, blocking the entrance to the school. "Well, don't think you're coming to my school and taking over. You're on my turf and don't you forget it."